The Tree House

Other books by Fionna Sheppard

Women's fiction:

The Weigh, the Piece and the Loaf

Watch for the author's new chicklit series *The Adventures of Stephie Wells* in 2015

Recipe books:

Gourmet Gluten Free Book One: Cakes and Cookies

This is the first in a series of eight books - the other are due early 2015

Children's stories:

The Quilt

Sukey's Hoya

The Tree House

By Fionna Sheppard

Chelmsford Publishing

The Tree House

Cover and interior design by Allison Sheppard

Published in New Zealand

Print version

ISBN: 978-0-9941161-0-9

Dedication

I dedicate this story to Lisa Nichols who inspired me on Power Week, Power Me to stop procrastinating and write the first draft, and to Lori Hamann who taught me to believe in myself and finish the process through to publishing.

Thank you both.

Acknowledgements

Thanks must go first to Stephen Walsh for everything, and to Bev Stevens at DesignIT, and Liz Gasparini in Melbourne for the help, comment and editing. The story is so much better after all your work!

A big thank you to my son, Alex, my very first reader and sharp eyed critic, who picked up my errors and explained the words I had put a kiwi slant on when they needed to be Americanised. You were a great help, and I really appreciate the time you spent doing this for me, Alex. I miss you. The internet is great, but being nearer would be better.

Huge thanks also to Allison Sheppard for her super cover image which conveys Boy's home so perfectly and her interior design. Alli, you rock and I love having a working relationship with you as well as our special mother/daughter link.

Contents

Prologue: 1982

I am an old man now. My wife and I sit out on the porch in the late summer sunshine, rocking in our chairs on the porch looking at the view. As I sit and reflect, it becomes the same porch, the same scene I saw as a boy. The same way I remember my grandparents, and my parents, too, looking across the valley in northern Maine, right below the mountains, in front of the forest. My forest.

Much of the forest has now gone. Logging trucks pass daily and the air is filled with noise. Protection for the wild animals is disappearing acre by acre as the land is cleared to become more farms, more houses, industry. The small farming community I grew up in is now a busy town. Railway lines track around the state, and getting places is so simple now compared to when I was young. Not that we go anywhere. We are content. My wife and I enjoy the solitude of our smallholding, the simple pleasures of lambs and calves in spring, of tending the flowers and the vegetables, and savouring the fruit from the orchard, first planted by my grandfather.

In my hands I hold my journals. Plain, brown notebooks, worn at the edges, pages inside covered with my childish writing and my drawings and sketches. Eight numbered journals, from 1905 to 1909, that chronicled my life as I moved from a boy of twelve into man of sixteen. Four years that formed me, made me who I am today.

I open the first journal, and right away, I am that boy again. I can still see him, feel him. I'm still him, even though my old bones groan, protesting as I sit or stand. Inside, as I read, I'm twelve years old again.

Who would have thought seventyfive years could pass so quickly?

Chapter One: Sorrows and Remembrances

I left home in the year of my twelfth birthday. It was sunny and clear, four days after school had ended for the summer vacation. I liked school, with its numbers and drawing and woodwork and writing, but I loved summer. I spent all winter longing for the sun to return after having hidden behind clouds and snow for so many months. Every now and then the wind would blow away the grey and give me just a tantalising peek to show me that the sun still was up in the sky, planning its comeback.

I was almost twelve years, three months old. In the bathroom mirror, old and losing its silvering, I saw my eyes, fringed with dark lashes: my mother's clear sky blue eyes. My mother's face, although thinner at the jawline with a small scar under my bottom lip. Brown hair, with a rough and ragged cut now that I trimmed it myself with the scissors from the kitchen drawer. A thin boy, not tall, wiry. A boy grown too big for his clothes, with a hint of what he might become as a grown man.

It was two years, two months and twenty three days since my mother died from the monster that ate her up from the inside until she was not much bigger than a tiny, helpless embryo. I couldn't bear to see the sadness in her eyes, and neither could my father. He wrote away to a catalogue and bought her a delicate flower, a pale, pale pink orchid, growing in a white china pot rimmed with gold. The mailman brought the box one day, and from then the pot sat on the small table beside her place on the porch, so they were both out of the wind, but still felt the warmth from the early spring sun. Father had tended to her so carefully, just as if she was that delicate flower. He would cook for her, tempting morsels of food, but in the end even chicken soup was too much.

Each sunny day, father would carry her out onto the white painted porch, wrapped in a gaily-patterned quilt, and place her gently on grandma's creaky old rocking chair, well padded with cushions. Mother would rock gently as she gazed out at our world around her. A world of fields and trees, mountains, animals.

Like a little bird, she was. We found a little baby bird once fallen from a tree, alive but scarcely and despite all our care it failed to thrive. Its mother would have pushed it from the nest to learn to fly, mother said. I asked her why, when it wasn't ready. She had shrugged her shoulders and said that was the way of things in the bird world. I think Mother was just like that little bird. She too left us before she was ready. Looking back now, I guess in a way father did the same to me – pushed me from the nest before I was ready. Maybe that's the way of things in the world of people as well.

I remember the day she left us. It's etched in my mind: the blue of the sky reflecting mother's eyes, the few soft billowy clouds overhead. The fresh-grown smell of the early spring grass. The day before my tenth birthday. I was sitting on a cushion on the top step of the porch just across from mother, leaning against the post, reading aloud from the book she had handed me. Father was in the other wicker chair, rocking, rocking, listening, as I read the words out loud. I reached the end of the chapter, and looked up to ask if she wanted me to turn over the page and continue. She smiled at me, sighed, once, and her eyes closed. Her lashes fluttered and were still.

For the longest time, father and I sat and looked at her, willing the quilt covering her tiny body to rise and fall, to show us she had just fallen asleep. But there was no movement. We sat and looked at each other. The anguish in his face was palpable. I expect mine echoed it. Father closed his eyes, wrapped mother in his arms and cried and cried. I tiptoed away, not wanting to see his pain, or have him see mine.

I remember everything. The nodding, yellow-faced daffodils in the garden lining the edge of the porch, green leaves thrusting up from the ground. The sound of lambs looking for their mothers. The soft moo and the slow creak of wood as the cow pushed hard against the fence to grab at the sweet grass on the other side. Time stopped for a moment.

That was the last day I can recall father ever looking at me with love. From then on, if he ever actually looked at me, his face was smeared with anger and grief and his eyes were dead. As if he had left this plane, but his body still went through the motions of being human. If you could call it human. Mostly though, he just looked past me, to something only he could see.

The day after the burial, after mother was committed to the cold brown earth under the tree on the little knoll in the cemetery, and the neighbours had gone home, father walked down the road from our house and into the saloon in the village. And after that, he mostly stayed there, each day sitting at the bar or lying across the bar – coming home late at night after the publican threw him out, albeit gently, as if he understood the grief. Staggering down the road, up the drive to the farmhouse, his hat askew, coat half off, boots partly tied up. When he got in the door, if I hadn't made myself scarce, father would methodically remove his belt from his old, greying, tweed trousers and thrash me with it till he ran out of energy and fell onto the sofa in the front room. My mother's beautiful raspberry velvet sofa upholstered with bronze studs that had been her mother's, and was her pride and joy. That was another thing I couldn't bear – the heedless destruction of my mother's belongings. If he loved her so much, why couldn't he treasure what she had left behind? Eventually I had given up trying to reason, to understand, to communicate. I was grieving too. The first time father hit me I was shocked, not understanding. But soon I learned to keep away, hide in my room or outside until I was sure he had fallen asleep. Often he found me anyway, and I wore many bruises and cuts to school. No one commented. I guess they figured it out for themselves.

The house became a shambles. I tried my best to tend the animals, to cook meals, sweep the floors. Even so, everything was falling apart. I went to school each day, but didn't do so well. I was sad and lonely and alone. A small boy without nurturing. My Aunt Sally came, shouted at father, and took me to stay with her, but for the whole three weeks I was away I pined for the farm, I missed my mother so much, my father too.

The children at the town school I attended mocked my country ways and I was relieved when Aunt asked me if I'd rather go back home than stay with her. I nodded, and the following day she brought me back to the farm. And I stayed there, putting up with the abuse, until I felt strong enough, brave enough, to make a change in my life.

I began to prepare to undertake the last part of my plan. I thought about all I would need for leaving home, and collected together some of my belongings, stuffing everything in an old cotton bag.

My old green oiled-cotton sleeping bag. Mother had made it for me on her old Singer treadle sewing machine. She filled it with the feathers from the ducks that had shared our orchard, garden and backyard before they became our dinner. The ducks waddled around in the yard and slept in the fowl house with the hens and an old, scrawny rooster who could – and did – still perform loudly, daily. I had helped her with measuring the fabric, and stuffing in the feathers – that is, after I had blown them around the room in a feather snowstorm. Mother laughed as I was covered with down, then made me clean it all up and stuff the feathers in the bag where they were supposed to go, before she finished the stitching.

The roasting dish I would pack last. Father would not use it, he didn't cook any more, but I still attempted to cook a meal each day. I'd eat my share, and leave a plate for father, but most times it went to the hens the next day. On Sundays, before mother left us, we would often have a roast duck. Mother would stand at the wood range, searing the bird, and draining off the fat into the old wide-mouthed glass jar, before stuffing the duck with breadcrumbs and sausage meat. I loved to watch the ritual. She would put the duck in the battered old black roasting dish to cook, adding a cup or so of water, potatoes, parsnips and sweet potato. Some black pepper and a handful of salt from the bowl on the bench, and into the thumping hot oven. The range was always hot when my mother was alive. It cooked our food and heated our water and made the kitchen toasty on those frosty winter nights when everything was still, sharp, clear, not a breath of wind. If I went outside and huffed, some nights I could make a brilliant sparkling ball of cold air that would last a couple of seconds, then disappear.

The range was only ever warm now if I lit the fire myself, chopping the wood up into small pieces, and feeding it, along with the pine cones I collected from the forest. I would wheel them home in the barrow and dump them into the wood box. The lid of the box was heavy and hard to lift when I was ten, but by the time I was twelve I had grown a lot taller, and much stronger, and it seemed easy.

I couldn't recall when I had last taken a bath. Or when my father had either. Instead, each day I filled the sink with hot water and washed myself there, standing on an old towel, using my mother's pink face cloths. She had twelve of them in the linen press, and twelve hand towels, twelve bath towels, the same. In one corner they had a monogram: JLR de W. Julietta Louise Rose de Wittinger. My mother. My beautiful, warm, smart, happy, serene, mother. Twelve pairs of white linen sheets and pillowcases, greying now, without mother to measure the bleach into the washing machine and swish water and sheets back and forth, back and forth, in the big enamel bowl, around the agitator, before she fed them through the wringer into the big concrete wash tub to be rinsed. Then back through the wringer again – twice – and into the laundry basket, which I would carry outside before helping her hang the linen onto the long wire clothes line and straightening the wooden prop, cut into a vee at the top, which pushed the line up high into the breeze.

I took two pillowcases and two pairs of her sheets for my leaving pile. Mostly for her smell that lingered in the linen cupboard. Meadow-sweet and fresh, with a touch of rose and lavender from the sachets she made each summer and put in the cupboard.

Salt, baking soda, toothbrush. I put the salt and baking soda in a jar, mixed together, making my toothpaste like mother always had.

Some soap. I stole the soap from mother's drawer in her room, where she kept the box with her clothes. It smelled of lavender, of her. Soft and smooth and pale. There were three round soaps in the box, with a purple ribbon tied around each one, holding in the purple tissue paper. The ribbon had a transfer stuck on it, with a drawing of lavender, to hold the package all together. I took the box as well, to keep me remembering.

A yellow and black box of thick white candles. The box always sat on the top shelf of the pantry cupboard next to the red boxes of long-tapered matches that Mother preferred for lighting the range. The candle box had four whole candles in it and three broken ones. I left the broken ones on the shelf. I took two boxes of the matches. And two cans of baked beans together with two of spaghetti.

A bag of small new potatoes from the garden.

The other items on my list, those I was still using all the time, would be the last to pack:

My pillow. Also made by my mother, with more feathers, encased in a piece of blue worn out shirt of father's that she had cut up and stitched into a casing, nothing ever wasted.

My clothes – which weren't much, as I had grown tall since she left. Without my mother to sew new shirts and cut down my father's trousers into pants for me, I looked a little like a scarecrow. Mother always made my pants too long in the leg, so I could grow into them, and for a while I'd have to roll the bottoms up. And then, suddenly, all in one day it seemed, I'd have grown into them. Now, I'd grown out of them.

Two pairs of pants. Two shirts, one a warm red flannel, and the other a blue and grey checked shirt mother had sewn for my tenth birthday, with room to let out the sleeves and the side seams and extra-long for me to grow to meet it.

A jersey, that mother knitted for my eleventh birthday but wasn't there to see me in it.

When the pain got too bad and she couldn't manage to use the sewing machine or even work magic with her knitting needles any longer, Mother had wrapped the shirt and the jersey into separate packages, with the dates on them, and had given them to me. She made me promise to leave them unopened till each birthday. The checked shirt I couldn't bear to look at, the day of her burial, my tenth birthday. I just left it in my cupboard. The jersey she made for me being eleven was dark green, with a grey zigzag pattern across the front and back, and grey around the vee neck and on the cuffs. It was too big when I put it on for the first time, on my eleventh birthday. I cried so much that I thought the jumper was blue, not green, and I put it away. When I took it out of the drawer to pack it into my bag, I was surprised. It fitted me, almost. Mother must have figured out how much I would grow over a year or two.

Socks, underwear. My jacket. A man's oilskin coat, a bit too big for me right now, but I would need it when the weather changed. My hat, warm and woolly, with stripes of all colours of left-over wool that my mother wove in a braided pattern with her needles. One pair of shoes, and the work boots that I wore on the farm.

The shoes had been my Uncle William's, mother's brother. He used to send all his old shoes – many hardly worn at all – I think it was his way of helping out without incurring the wrath of my father, without shaming him, so he wouldn't glower in his chair, thinking people thought he couldn't provide properly for his family. He could, of course he could. Before my mother died, that was.

Before, when my father was a happy man. He kissed my mother good morning and told her how much he loved her, every day, without fail, as he went out the back door. He would pause to put on his boots, and then sneak back in to wrap his arms around her tiny waist and kiss her again, loudly, a big smack, on her cheek. She would flap him away with her hands, scolding him for wearing his boots indoors, but with a big smile, so full of love on her face, her big blue eyes twinkling and crinkling in the corners. He whistled as he went about his work, the farm was immaculate. The grain was always of good quality, the cows fat and placid, chewing their cud in the fields, the lambs in spring bouncing about the green green grass in the orchard where he moved the ewes for lambing because it provided good shelter and was close to the house.

Now, the neighbours lent a hand when they could; the farmer from next door on his tractor chugging along in our fields cutting the hay, the man from across the road tending to our stock, both helping us after they had finished their own work for the day. My father seemed oblivious.

I gathered the pile of things I'd been collecting from inside the house and carefully hid them in a corner of the barn, as I got closer to the day. L day. Leaving Day. I wasn't sure of the exact day I would leave, but I knew it was coming closer.

Chapter Two: Creation

I had made up my mind a fair while before. I said to myself, the next time father hits me, I'm going to walk out the door and never come back. I started getting ready in a general way a long time before it all came clear in my mind about what I was going to do. And how I would do it.

I had found the tree in the old forest behind our farm when I was small. It was huge – especially to a small boy of six – but I instantly knew that we were going to have a life-long connection. Of course, back then it was just fun, a secret place, something that a small boy with no siblings and few friends kept to himself. I paced around the tree. When I was six, it took sixteen of my small boy strides to circle the trunk. I don't know how old that made the tree, but I knew it was very old. When I craned my neck and looked up up, I couldn't see the sky, just a mass of branches with spiny bits all over them. I learned from one of the books in my father's shelf that it was a kind of pine tree. A redwood. Sequoia sempervirens. There were some other trees like it in the forest, but not many. Mostly the forest was full of trees with a sort of blueish colour on the branches, thicker branches and very dense. The branches of those trees came right down to the ground, good for hiding in but they didn't grow so tall. They were the kind people cut for Christmas trees.

My tree was different; it had very thick bark, reddish, and the trunk grew straight up. The lower branches were quite a long way off the ground, especially for a boy who wasn't very big, and I had to throw a rope over the bottom one to haul myself up. When I was six, even throwing a rope that high was too hard. I tried banging in some nails with my hammer, to use as a rudimentary form of steps, but the wood was so hard the nails sprang back fiercely and I hurt my thumb. With a lot of practice, I taught myself how to throw a rope up and eventually got myself up to the lower branches.

After that, as often as I could, I would head down the road that ran past our farm and turn into the forest. It took me more than half an hour to reach the tree from the end of the road when I was little.

By the time I got to my eighth birthday, I could climb right to the top of the tree. I had improved my rope throwing; even so, it was still quite an effort to get up. Over the years, the tree had grown a little bit more, although I had grown too, and I was sure it was more than the tree, because the lower branches were definitely more accessible. That was such an exciting day, my eighth birthday – I remember my heart pumping as I reached higher and higher in the branches. It seemed to take a long long time, as I chose each move carefully, a handhold here, a sturdy branch that would support my weight as my next foothold. I climbed and climbed. I felt like Jack, in the Beanstalk story. If I looked down I got a bit scared, so I stopped looking down and focused on climbing up. When I arrived at the top and peered out, I could see for miles. Blue hills in the distance across a sea of trees in one direction, mountains, much closer, in another. A big lake far away. About half way up the tree, maybe 50 feet I reckoned although I never knew for sure, where the branches started to spread wide, I had noticed there was a big clear flattish space. It seemed like maybe some of the branches of the tree had been trimmed straight across, or had broken more likely, long ago – maybe even a hundred years ago when it was still young – and then left to grow again.

Whatever had occurred, the space in the branches would make a wonderful place for a tree fort I thought. And so I made one. I kept it to myself, not telling anyone at school, or father even, but I did confide in my mother. It was our secret. At first, it was a rough hut banged together and not waterproof – in fact not anything proof, more a rough shelter.

No one ever asked me what I was doing. I guess because I was quiet, polite, and not very big for my age people generally left me alone. I laboured away, building my fort, which became my hut, which turned into a tree house. At night, I dreamed about it, and once I could read well enough, became engrossed in the stories about tree houses mother found for me in books on her shelf or at the library in the village where I went to school. My tree house. It was six feet one way, eight feet the other and seven feet high. I worked out the space, then calculated all the measurements at school. It became a project; I made a model of it in woodwork class when I was ten, and got an A pass for it. I never let on that it was to become a real building.

When I made the decision that I would run away from father and live there, I began to hurry the process, gathering pieces of wood – old fence posts, cut off pieces from the local sawmill that the men let me take home probably thinking it was for firewood, or for small repairs around our farm. I let them think that. The sawmill was a constant source of materials. I found some good long pieces of corrugated iron, and as the L-day got closer, I stole a piece of siding off the back of the barn and hauled that into the forest, too.

Before I started to build the tree house proper after mother died, not just the rough fort I had created, I had to figure out how I could get everything up the tree. That took me quite some time. I created a simple pulley system, using an old winch and hook that had hung in the barn, and I wove and knotted myself a sturdy rope ladder. I painstakingly tied the wood and the other building materials securely, piece by piece, and winched them up, slowly. Each load that I hauled into the forest, tied with rope and pulled up into the tree brought the project nearer and nearer to completion.

I laid the floor first, plank by plank. My woodwork teacher had taught me amazing things when I was designing and creating my model at school. All I had to do was ask a question and off he'd go, drawing as he talked. I suppose it was such a change for him, having a kid in the class who asked and was really interested in learning. He taught me to mitre corners, make pegs, drill holes, cut angles, not knowing how quickly I'd put those lessons into practice.

After the floor was down, I started on the framing and the roof. It took me ages to get it right. Pieces would keep falling down off my platform and I'd have to haul them all the way back up. It was frustrating, till I figured out what I was doing wrong. When I made my model, I had built the sides first, and sat the roof on the top – and that's how I was building it. But for the real thing, I needed a frame at the top, anchored in the corner timbers, that would enable the roof to go on. Once I had done that, putting up the walls became easy. I used my granddad's old tools in the forest, and the lathe and school equipment in woodwork class. I drilled the holes, banged in the pegs I had made, and was delighted when it all held together.

Once the walls were up, I made the roof from more planks that I covered with corrugated iron. I extended the iron over the edge of the frame to provide better protection from the weather. Now I had a room with a floor and a roof and partly open sides. I poked around the community, asking the farmers if they had old bits and pieces of wood or ply, or indeed anything they didn't need. The men at the sawmill gave me all sorts of stuff after I lied about my intentions and asked them for materials to fix the hen house. I even found two old window frames with unbroken glass and fitted them into the walls, after quite a lot of manoeuvring and adjustments. Getting the windows up into the tree took hours and hours it seemed, and I was so relieved not to have broken the glass panes in the process. The door, too, took some working out, but I eventually figured out how to build that. Then all I needed were hinges and a handle, and I helped myself to those hanging on the hen house door. There were so many holes in the henhouse walls that the hens didn't bother to use the door anyway. I would have taken the henhouse door itself, if it hadn't been so ramshackle.

Once the tree house was built, the wind didn't actually whistle through the frame, but it wasn't very weathertight and I knew it would be awfully cold up there come winter. I nailed empty old wool bales against the inside walls and stuffed wool into them, thinking the extra layers might make the room warmer. If it kept sheep warm in the snow, then maybe it would work to keep me warm too. And it worked well. By poking wool into the frame around the door, I'd substantially reduced the cold air weaselling its way in through the cracks. Then I took an old horse blanket from the barn to act as a curtain over the door and covering the frame. Old sacks nailed across the top became my blinds for the two windows, tied up with strings.

My idea to use wool and the wool bales for extra warmth excited me. I thought about how it could be adapted for houses, to keep the heat in during the freezing winters. And then I noticed during the summer as I completed my building it actually kept the small room cooler in the heat. At first, I couldn't figure it out – why outside on the deck was so hot, but inside, when I arrived, often during the hottest part of the day, the house was cooler inside. Once I realised that the wool acted as insulation from the worst of the hot or cold weather I was amazed. It truly seemed a miracle to me. No doubt sheep never thought about their woolly coat at all – at least not till it was shorn off each year.

The neighbours were so kind to me after mother died. I will never forget that. One day in early summer, the year I was getting ready to leave home, the farmer next door saw me trying to herd the sheep into the ramshackle pen for shearing and came across to help. It didn't take long, we only had five sheep and they weren't in great condition. More suited to the pot than anything the farmer said, and I had to agree with him.

After we had finished the task, I took one partly full bale to make a bed for my tree house. It was quite comfortable, although only just long enough to lie down. If I lay straight, my feet hung off the end.

Early in the spring, as soon as the ground was soft enough for planting, I dug over the vegetable garden and prepared the ground with watered-down chicken poop and cow manure. The farmer next door said if I shovelled the cow manure from his wintering barn I could have as much as I wanted for the garden, and a few dollars, besides. My goodness, it was an awful job. I'd come home smelling so bad, and have to scrub myself clean every night. But I made me some money, and I had four big sacks of manure, which I dug into the earth before I sowed my seeds: carrots, beans, cabbages, cauliflower, turnips...anything I could get my hands on. I tended the garden extra well all that summer.

What I didn't know, was how to manage cooking and heating once I was living in the tree house. Father and I had often been out trapping when mother was there, so I knew how to catch animals, and prepare them, too. But how would I cook them? I couldn't make a fire in the tree, I reasoned, but what about some sort of an enclosed wood-burner arrangement? It all seemed too difficult.

There was also the issue about storing the wood after I'd chopped it, in a place so no one would find it, but I could access it easily. I took an axe from the tools in the barn, early on, and each day would cut a little more wood for my pile. The fallen branches from trees near to mine in the forest were an endless source of wood. I stole a shovel from the barn as well. A deep hole, dug not far from the base of the tree – my long drop I called it – became a crude lavatory, carefully concealed, but easy to access.

I kept thinking about the fireplace situation, and how I'd keep warm. The farmhouse was cold enough in winter – even with the range burning – and I knew without some form of heating I would freeze in my tree house as the forest would be far colder. I spent time in the library, looking up old woodworking books and magazines, searching for tips on making a fireplace, and eventually figured out a simple way that I thought would work and be safe. I didn't want the tree to catch on fire.

One day, when I was poking about in a disused shed at the back of the sawmill down the road, I came across an old piece of chimney. Then I struck gold, finding an old cylinder with a triangular piece attached to it. With a little adjustment, I managed to fit one end of the chimney column onto it, and I cut a hole on one side to make a fire cavity. Together with a baking rack from mother's oven, I had created something I could cook on. Now all I needed was a metal plate big enough to put under it, to stop ash and embers from falling on the floor of the tree hut. Eventually I found the perfect solution using the lid from the small grain silo. Father hadn't planted grain for the last two years, so the silo was empty. The lid was sturdy, the right size and shape, and not too big for me to carry. It had a deep lip that would hold the embers effectively and handles on the side.

Getting the chimney up into the tree and securing it was the next task, and then I finished by cutting a hole through the wall to join it all up together. Fitting the silo lid and the baking rack together and sealing up the joins so the chimney didn't leak smoke or ash took ages, but eventually it was finished, and it didn't look too bad, either. I admired my handiwork, sad that I couldn't go home and tell my mother how our secret was coming along. Some days though, I was sure she was there, in the whisper of the trees, in the long fingers of sun, shining through the branches, in the bird song, I heard her, and I thought she could see what I was doing.

I was nearly done. I had a house to live in with a strong roof, a fireplace I could cook in, a bucket I could wash in, a bed, a table and some shelving. A lockable door that closed tight, windows that could open. Best of all, it was mine.

I went through my mental checklist and ticked everything off. Now it was just a matter of time.

Once the construction was complete I used the tree house as my getaway space during the day after I had completed my farm chores, but I didn't spent any nights there even when I began the task of moving in my gear. Mostly because I was afraid someone would notice my absence, although who was there to notice? Father wouldn't I was sure.

The day before I finally left home my father came in late, breathing fire and fumes, calling for me, his eyes glazed and teary. I didn't try to hide from him, this time, as I usually did. Heart thumping, afraid, but I knew this was it. So I stood there in the kitchen and answered him when he stepped through the doorway and yelled for me.

I'm here father. I made dinner, it's on the stove. I flinched when he hit me the first time, the second, the third. At first, I cowered back, just as he expected me to, just as I had all the other times, when the belt came off his trousers and he flexed it at me. A sting across my legs, my chest, my face. With each thwack I tried to cover my head, protect myself. And then finally the courage came. I stood tall. I won't accept this anymore, I said to myself, I am stronger than he is, and bigger. I can stop this. I can. I will. At the next rush father made towards me, arm raised, belt buckle dangling, I stepped aside, and grabbed his arm. It registered somewhere in the back of my mind how strong I had become, building the tree house, hauling materials, climbing up and down, up and down the tree trunk. Enough, father. Enough. He stared at me in a fugue, pulled back from me and raised his arm again. I grabbed at it a second time, forced his hand down. Enough, I shouted. I am not responsible for her death. Neither are you.

I saw the look of shock on his face, the recognition that I was nearly an adult, that I had the strength to force his arm away, force him away from me. He hadn't realised how much I had grown. I was now his same height, although I was only twelve.

I stared at him, willing him to look at me, acknowledge me, something. Anything.

Father turned away, refusing to look at me. He stomped over to the range, picked up the plate of food waiting for him and flung it violently against the wall. The plate shattered. Spaghetti trickled down the wall, red rivulets, white worms. I ran outside, but father didn't come after me. I hid in the barn for some time, before venturing back inside, listening for his snores that made it safe for me to return. He was asleep as usual, on the sofa, mother's beautiful, raspberry velvet sofa, smeared with mud from his shoes and worse.

I took a deep breath. I propped the note I had written him, saying I had gone to stay with Aunt Sally, on the table beside the clock. I walked around the house quietly and picked up the last few things on my list. I took the dollars I had earned from the farmer, and the few that were in the jar on the mantelpiece. I took the photo of mother from beside my bed. And before I could feel scared, or have second thoughts about what I was doing, I was out the door. Goodbye, father, I whispered. Goodbye.

Chapter Three: New Beginning

I loaded up my sled with the stuff already hidden in the shed and the last things I had grabbed from the house, and pulled my life, my belongings, myself, away from all that I knew. How I would survive, I had no real idea. I just knew this was the time; this was the right thing to do. Aunt Sally would have taken me in again, but what would I do in a town? The children at the town school would mock my country ways, just as they had done during the few weeks I stayed with my aunt after mother went. I didn't want that. I wanted my mother, but that wasn't possible. I made up my mind that I didn't want anyone, didn't need anyone. While I had been waiting, expecting this day for some time, the beating I had taken this time had numbed me in an odd, unexpected way. However, the reality was still shocking.

Tears fell unheeded and my nose was snotty as I pulled my sled away from the barn. From the farmhouse that had been my home. Away from everything that was comfortable, familiar. I felt the blood from the wound where father's belt buckle caught me on my forehead still trickling down the side of my face, and I knew I'd be sore and bruised in the morning. But now, tonight, the energy I needed to get me away filled my body, kept my heart pounding, an adrenalin rush. The stars were out, thick as crystals encrusting the sky in the country night air, no town lights to dim them and just a sliver of moon. I could identify many of the stars; they were my friends, they taught me direction. That night I didn't have time to stargaze. I was sure father wouldn't wake until the morning, but I was afraid someone might see me and I was anxious to get into the shelter of the trees.

I hauled my sled along the road, moving as quickly as I could. I was free. No one would hit me ever again, I vowed. I never had to see father again. There was a part of me that was sad at that realisation, but the other part said that's it, I have to create a new, different life, keep myself safe.

The forest was in total darkness, and the trees loomed eerily. I hadn't been there in the night before now, but my feet knew the way and unerringly guided me to my new home. I uncovered the rope which fed both the pulley and the rope ladder from its hiding place, and began the task of taking up the last of the provisions, my clothes and the rest of the stash from the shed. It didn't take long – I had done this so many times before the process seemed automatic, even in the dark.

Finally I was done. I anchored the pulley in its hiding place, well hidden by trees and rocks, climbed the ladder, pulled it up, and hooked it onto a branch. Hello house, I'm home, I said to myself with a wry grin.

I opened my little door, and walked inside. I had left a candle in a candlestick on top of the fireplace, in preparation. I lit it carefully, and looked about me.

My body was sore, my heart was too, but I felt cocooned by my little house, it was warm and cosy and safe. Up here, no one could reach me, no one could hit me, and no one could hurt me. I put the photo of mother on one of the shelves I had built around the walls to keep my clothes, provisions, and books off the floor. The small space meant everything had to be tidy and organised, and I was careful not to leave anything too near my fireplace. I'd tested the fire and chimney a couple of times since I had installed it, and I felt confident it was reasonably safe and secure. No smoke or ash leaked out into the room and it drew well; still, I was cautious – a fire up the tree would be fatal.

It was full summer, not nearly cold enough for a fire at night unless I was cooking, and I had some fresh food to last a few days. Smoke in the forest in the summer might attract some attention, even this far away from the road, so I'd have to eat whatever I could find that didn't need cooking. Not far from the tree was a meandering stream, cold as it came straight down from the mountains behind the farms, fast running in the spring, and always fresh and sweet. I had an idea to use it to keep food cool, tie a sack with a bottle in it to keep cool, or even rabbit that I trapped, but discounted that early on. Other than planting a big vegetable garden, I hadn't really thought out the food situation – my focus had been on getting the house built. I thought there would be berries around, or nuts that I could eat, but I didn't know enough to find ones that wouldn't poison me.

I washed my face with the water in my bucket, staining mother's pink facecloth with the crusted blood from the cut on my head, took off my outer clothes and climbed into my wool bale bed.

That first night was sad, but I wasn't lonely and I wasn't afraid. In the dark, starry night, I considered all the things I had forgotten earlier. Like enough food for years, not just one season. Like learning. I had brought some books with me, but I would soon be bored with those, and want more. Moreover, what would I do long term? How long would I, could I, live here? What would happen when people realised I had gone? Would they worry? Would they search for me? How long before father contacted Aunt Sally to see how I was? What would happen if or when they found me? I began to sob quietly. I was twelve years old. Mother was gone and no amount of wishing would bring her back, or make father become the man he used to be before she died. I knew he would never be, could never be, that father again. I would never feel his arms around me with affection, never work alongside him on the land as he whistled, strong and happy. I was now on my own and it was up to me to make a new life for myself. How I fashioned it would decide my fate.

I lay on my little mattress on the floor, my head on mother's monogrammed pillowcase that covered my old pillow, mother's sheets smelling sweet around me, warmed by the extra feather comforter mother had kept in the sandalwood chest in the spare room. In case visitors came.

I recalled how, whenever she lifted the lid of the chest, the pungent odour would waft about – colouring the air with dreams of Asian rain forests, she'd tell me. Now the scent lingering in the fabric comforted me, bringing back warm happy memories of my mother. In my mind, I saw her, moving about the farmhouse with purpose, shaking a cushion, smoothing the tablecloth, wiping the kitchen counter, stirring a pot on the range.

I fell asleep at last, tears finally drying on my cheeks. In my dreams, she came to me and I felt her cool hand on my brow, brushing back the hair falling across my forehead, whispering goodnight my boy, I love you more than all the waves in the sea, all the stars in the sky. In the distance, an owl hooted and all was peaceful.

Chapter Four: Reality

The dappled sunlight through the windows woke me early the next morning. In the dark I hadn't thought to untie the strings holding up the sacks that were my curtains. I opened the door and peered out. So high in the trees, all I could see across and up were more trees, branches, and when I looked down it suddenly seemed such a long way to the ground. Yet I had climbed up and down the ladder so many times I had forgotten just how far down it actually was.

I listened carefully. No sound of humans. In all the years since I found the tree and made my house, I hadn't met a single person in the forest. I thought that maybe no one came here. Certainly, I had never seen any other kids playing in the trees. I wondered why, before remembering that there were no young people in the cluster of farms around our place other than myself – they had all grown up, moved away. With no work here or nearby, other than farm labouring, the young people moved away to make their lives. Just parents or grandparents left to tend the smallholdings.

Until this summer, I had caught the bus to school each day from the main road, two miles from home. If I missed the bus, it was a further three miles to school in the village. It was a good walk in the summer, but in the winter with the cold, wet, snow and winds howling through the valley, it became a hard slog. The dozen or so children at the school came from all around the area, and we didn't tend to socialise, other than at school events. I always had chores to do after school, and I'd rush through them so I could go into the forest. I guess the other kids all had chores too.

No sound of animals, either. The forest was reputed to have bears, and I remember father had said that when he was young, mountain lions had occasionally come down into the farming community, but I hadn't seen or heard any in my lifetime. I recalled father telling me one day, years back when we were walking through the trees, about the trappers last century that had cleaned out a lot of the wildlife in their search for bearskins. Trophy hunters, too, had taken many of the lion and deer, driving the animals further into the mountains. The Indians had once trapped for skins in the forest taking them upriver to the town to trade. I didn't know if they still did that. I hadn't seen any Indians either, although I knew a tribe had a summer camp not too far away in a lush valley.

I desperately needed to pee. The easiest solution was to lean over the ledge that I euphemistically called a deck and urinate. So I did. There certainly wasn't anyone below, and no one anywhere to see, notice or comment. It became part of my morning ritual. I'd wake up, greet the morning and pee over the edge.

I woke up that first morning with the remnants of a dream still sticking in my mind. Unstructured images flashed in and out...memories of my mother and father in earlier, happier times, with me as a small child out in the fields laughing, having a picnic. My father in a checked flannel shirt, red braces holding up his rough tweed work pants and a battered straw hat with a ribbon and a feather around the brim; mother in a soft yellow full skirted dress and a big sun hat, strands of her hair falling out of the loose bun she usually wore. I was barefoot, in little blue shorts, red braces and a shirt just like my father's, clutching a bunch of scarlet poppies in my sticky little hand. Laughing and running about playing catch me. My father pulling me up in his strong arms and throwing me into the air, catching me as I shrieked, more, father, more, each time he'd go to set me down. Mother opening the big basket, spreading out the faded blue checked cloth, a smile on her face. The warm sun on my face.

The happiness lingered after the dream faded, but then it too disappeared and all the worries that had filled my brain last night came surging back. How was I going to live? How would I survive in the forest? I obviously couldn't go to school, because it wouldn't take much for people to know I was hiding somewhere. So how would I learn everything I needed to know? What about food? I was constantly hungry. Sure, I had the fireplace set up and there were the vegetables back at the farm, but in reality was I going to be able to feed myself properly?

All these things I hadn't considered when building the tree house, being so full of angst over my father and sorrow over my mother, suddenly hit. The angst was good, at the time; it kept me going, working away on the building. Each nail I drove in, each peg I pounded took me away from the bitterness and in a funny way lessened the pain of it all.

However, the questions pounding in my brain now were quite relentless – would I stay here always? How would I earn money? Where could I get new clothes when I grew out of the clothes I had?

I sat on the ledge, the filtered sunlight dappling my head and shoulders, and thought hard. I'd write a list of questions I needed to figure out, and then ask for inspiration. As I got answers, I'd write them on the paper beside the question. I went back inside my house, and located the notebook I had brought with my belongings. I wrote down everything I'd been tossing around in my head. I was sure the inspiration wouldn't appear instantly, but I had myself a plan, and that seemed a good thing.

That first day passed very slowly, despite my busyness. I checked the outside of the house and banged in more nails where I felt any planks were less than secure. I arranged my supplies on the shelf: a bag of rice, a bag of sugar, an old saucepan and a frying pan with a lid, the roasting pan. A wooden spoon, a big metal spoon, a spatula, a can opener, a sturdy knife. Some carrots, half a dozen somewhat withered turnips from last season, a bag of onions, and my bag of potatoes - everything I had dug from my garden and stored in the shed waiting for the time. The cans of spaghetti and baked beans.

I set my books on another shelf, above the makeshift fold-down table I had fashioned from a small cupboard door I found in the barn and two hinges from the hen house nesting boxes. Propped up by a sturdy stick, the table worked just fine. Having done that, I looked around my new home. What else to do? The leftover pegs I had turned were ideal for hanging up my few clothes, my hat, my warm jacket, my oilskin coat. My shoes, my work boots sat on the floor by the door. The few other items that made up the rest of my wardrobe – sock, underwear and the like – I put in an old box.

Now the tidying was finished, what would I do next? I looked at my watch; an old one losing its silvering that had been my granddad's and lost a minute or two each week. Only two in the afternoon. I threw down the rope ladder and climbed to the ground, used the long drop, and decided to take myself for a walk in the forest. In all the years of coming here, once I had found the tree and started my building, I hadn't walked the area at all. I was so engrossed in my project that I had quite forgotten to explore my surroundings. And when I had been in the forest before, when I was little, I was with father, and intent on following his long strides. After securing the ladder, I found myself a sturdy stick – in case of wild animals – and set out, compass, a pencil and my notebook in my pocket, the latter in case I got some inspiration.

Before I left, I checked that the big pile of wood I had chopped into small pieces was safe. Hidden under an old tarpaulin I had covered with mossy rocks, the pile looked like it had always been there. In one corner was an opening, where I could pull out pieces of wood as I needed without making it obvious. It was intact; no animal had considered burrowing in. I'd need all that wood and more, I thought, once the winter came – and even in the summer, if I was to cook food at all. I worried if I'd have enough wood – and then realised, what a joke – I was surrounded by trees, pinecones, fallen branches. I had plenty of fuel within a few metres of the tall tree where my house perched way up high.

I walked east for quite a while, mostly following the stream; I figured I couldn't get lost if I did that. I was absorbed with my thoughts at first, and it was some time before I gradually became aware that I was climbing higher and higher. The trees started to thin out, and more rocky outcrops appeared. The vista was similar to the view that I could see whenever I climbed to the very top of my tree – just trees forever, distant blue hills, a big lake far away, and in front of me the mountains, soaring high, snow topped even in this hot summer.

I sat on the sun-warmed rocks and gazed around. My mother's voice, soft like I remembered, whispered so clearly in my ear that I jerked around to look. There was no one with me. Take out your notebook, she said and I did. I found the pencil and prepared to write. Address the first question, said her voice. I looked at my paper. How will I survive? was the first thing I had written. With joy, she instructed me to scribe, and so I did. I never thought to question, or wonder if it really was my mother talking to me. I felt sure it was, and with that knowing, everything seemed to shift and settle in my mind. She would help me. I could call on her; ask her whenever I needed an answer. Maybe she would help me ask the questions I didn't even know I should ask. We worked our way down the list. How will I eat? Eat sparingly of what you have, and in the evenings, at dusk, go back to the farm and pick fruit, pull the rest of the vegetables. Your father won't be cooking or gardening and you have planted so well, you won't want to waste any. In the winter, another solution will appear.

What about my education? Quietly make your way to the library and find the books you want to read. If you sit in a dark corner, no one will notice you. Pretend you have a magic cloak that makes you invisible – if you think you can't be seen, others will think the same.

What do I do if people start looking for me? No one will be looking for you. You left your father a note and he will not think to question it, or follow up with Aunt Sally. Mother laughed. She doesn't get on with her brother as you well know and isn't likely to come visiting or even write and ask how you are. If the teacher calls in, your father will say where you have gone, that is, if he's sober – and if he's not, the teacher will read the note on the table.

How long would I stay here? Until it's time to move on.

How would I earn money? I would need money for clothes, provisions, and other food. Solutions will appear when you need them.

There was silence after I finished my writing, and I became aware I was alone again. That is, if there really had been someone, something, here – but still, the answers which had felt so daunting this morning, appeared as if from nowhere, and my page was now filled with words. I read each question and answer again, and again, and felt a level of satisfaction.

The sun was starting its slow summer descent when I stood up and turned to the west, facing the way I had come. Down the hill I clambered and then followed the stream. Apart from a couple of squirrels, I had seen nothing that moved, heard nothing but the whisper in my ear. The forest was shady but the air was still so warm. I called thanks to the sky for the long hot summer, and walking faster than before began the journey back to my new home. Even so, it wasn't long before I realised I had travelled a fair distance getting to the rocky outcrop. More than two hours passed before I stood once again beside my tree. I retrieved the rope ladder from its hiding place and climbed up, tired now. Preparations for dinner required little effort – I opened a can of spaghetti and forked it out of the can into my mouth. It tasted wonderful. I thought about food, yet again. I'd have to cook some things during the day, to minimise the use of my candles. I looked again at the questions and the answers in my book. And I decided to keep a journal, writing every day, so that in the future – whatever it looked like – I could read and remember this time of my life. Maybe I'd even have a family one day, and could read my story to my children. I laughed at the fanciful notion, as I got ready for bed. I blew out the candle. Goodnight house, sleep tight.

Chapter Five: Wintering Over

That first day and night set the pattern of my life for the next three years. Of course, I didn't realise it at the time. I had found a way of living I could cope with. I had ideas. I would draw and write in my notebooks. I would educate myself. I would learn as much as I could. I dreamed of going to university, of maybe becoming an architect. I would make my mother proud. I would forget how my father had treated me.

The summer was long that year. I explored the forest, east, west, north, south. I could walk three hours in any direction – except towards the farming community – and still be in woodlands, though in the west the trees weren't as tall and the spaces more open. I saw the valley where an Indian camp was, but stayed well away. I found a sunny spot, high in the hills, with a patch of wild blueberries and in another place spotted summer sweet strawberries. I gathered pine cones, chopped more wood. Some nights, I'd sneak back to the farm, and gather the orchard fruit as it ripened, and pull the vegetables. The stream provided me with fresh, sweet water – to drink, to bathe in, to wash my clothes in (although not very often, I admit), to cook with – as well as a source of food. There were often fresh water crawlies and brook trout, which I'd catch and fry up whole in my frying pan, delicious. I tied a rope to a tree branch that hung over the stream and would swing out each morning, dropping into the freezing water, using mother's lavender soap to wash.

I looked carefully for any traces of animals – footprints, droppings. I was afraid that at any time a bear might shimmy up the tree and knock on my door. Of course, I thought that wasn't likely to happen, but still, it behoved me to be careful. One day out walking, about a month after I had been living in the forest, I heard scuffling, and came across a bear digging a den. The weather was hot, and she would dig, stop and pant, dig again. I studied her movements, fascinated, keeping my distance. The bear came across a big rock, and I watched with awe the way she managed the obstacle. She backed out of the den, smoothed the entry to make a gentler slope, and enlarged the entrance. Then she went in and rolled the rock out, and resumed her work. I marvelled at her skill, and was careful to note the area so I would be sure to avoid it in future wanderings. A mama bear is very protective of her cubs and I surely didn't want to get in the way by mistake...

Each day, carefully, I wrote in my book, recording the events. Even with minute writing to minimise the page usage, I was going to need several more notebooks for my journaling.

I wrote everything I could remember from when I decided to leave home. I wrote about mother, and father, too. I tried to put as much information in as I could, even when it seemed a little dull, even when it seemed outright boring. This was what my life was. This is what I wanted to remember.

I thirsted for knowledge. I wanted to learn more about building, about woods, all the different materials one could use to build. About the way a tall building was crafted so that it stood up straight and didn't fall over. I already knew a lot about weather, and wind and snow, being on a farm, but I wanted to know more. Did wind have much effect on how a building was built? I was enthused by the method of insulating walls I had invented and I wanted to know more, other ways. And about people, and why people did what they did when they were sad and hurting. Why it was different for each person. Why weren't we the same?

I decided to take the advice of my mother, my whisperer. I hadn't heard her whispering to me since my first day at the tree house, and as the days shortened, a sense of urgency came over me. I had to take the next step. So, one week day, wearing an old hat of my granddad's with a wide brim, I walked out to the road. No one was close by. In the distance, I saw the neighbouring farmer on his tractor, but it appeared safe to keep going. I turned left and travelled the five miles into the village. I made my way along the road behind the main street, surreptitiously looking about me to see if anyone was about. What if someone identified me? I kept my head down and fingers crossed, hoping to reach the library building without being accosted. It all seemed clear, and I scuttled in the main door. I skulked around, eventually finding a corner out of view of the main room that looked as if it had been set up, just for me. I smiled to myself. Maybe my whisperer had prepared it. The space was partially hidden by a narrow screen and received good light from a nearby window. A scarred desk pushed against the wall and an old battered chair with a slightly sagging brown leather seat and frayed rattan on the back made up my "office" as I decided to call it, and I could easily venture out to the shelves and look for specific books without being noticed.

For several days over the next two weeks, I went in early each day, always taking the back road, and sneaking in around the back way. I sat at the desk, on the battered chair, and read the books I took off the shelves, returning them to their rightful place each night. I hardly saw or heard a soul. No one seemed interested about looking in a murky old corner of the library – until about the sixth day, when I heard a faint psst! and I looked up from my book in fright. The librarian, with a twinkle in her eye, sidled in through the small gap left between the wall and the end of the screen. Hello, she whispered, can I help you with anything? I'm not here, I said, somewhat stupidly. Of course you're not, she nodded. But if you were, might I suggest you look at the school curriculum for this year, and leave me a list of books you might want? Or anything else that interests you?

I was dumbstruck. She just smiled at me so very kindly again, and disappeared, leaving a pile of papers stapled together on the corner of the desk – the school curriculum for my year, and for the two years ahead of me.

That was how the pattern of my days unfolded. Four days every week I'd get up with the sun, fix some breakfast, sweep the ashes from my fire into a tin pail, take a perfunctory wash in my bucket, brush my teeth and walk out to the road, after depositing the ashes down the long drop. I'd take the left fork and hurry to cover the distance into the library. There would be exercise books, pencils, and pens waiting on my desk, along with the books I had asked for, and the class work the librarian left for me. Asked, as in noting them down on a piece of paper and leaving it on the desk at the end of the day. I would do my assignments in the mornings, and then spend my afternoons with my nose stuck into any book that had taken my fancy as I browsed the shelves.

Each afternoon, just before the library closed, I put on my hat and coat and quietly left the building for the walk home. As I passed the farm, if I thought it was safe, if father wasn't there – and generally, he wasn't – I'd sneak into the vegetable garden and pull a few carrots, an onion, a cabbage, for my evening meal. Not every day, but maybe once or twice a week, and I would get enough to last me until the next time. Each time my heart would race, as I sidled around the back of the house, shimmied over the fence and ducked down, hoping to be invisible. Once back in the forest I'd release my breath. OK again this time I'd say to myself.

I jumped into the stream each day after the library, to have a proper wash. However, as the weather got colder, the washes got shorter, and after a while, I depended on my bucket to keep clean. I was getting into the ways of cooking over the fireplace. I would generally cook a pile of vegetables, enough for dinner, and to have leftovers for breakfast. Sometimes I cooked rice, and put vegetables with that. I'd sit out on the tiny deck outside, feet dangling over the edge, eating my food and watching the light change from gold to red to purple as the sun dropped behind the hills in the west.

I hadn't started trapping yet. On the days I didn't go into town I'd wander through the forest, and gather the nuts, leaves and berries I had learned from my library reading were OK to eat, or head for the blueberry patch even though it was late in the summer and the fruit were wizened. I would put them in the pot with rice and some sugar and make myself a sweet treat.

When I was at the library, the librarian would occasionally put her head around the screen and smile then vanish. She would leave me a note if she needed to say anything, and I would write back. I seldom noticed anyone else there either. I didn't stop to think that it seemed a bit weird. After all, I was invisible. Just as my whisperer had suggested to me, I pretended I wore an invisible cloak when I entered the library, and I guess it worked.

I raced through my prescribed schoolwork, and then indulged in books about building, architecture, trees and plants. I learned about famous architects, about Roman and Greek structures and civilisation. I read about the lost city of Atlantis, and the aqueducts of the Romans. I learned about the kinds of wild animals that lived in the community, how to identify them. Father had taught me a lot when we had been trapping, I now realised, but I wanted to learn more.

One day there was a note on my desk when I arrived at the library, covering an examination paper. The librarian looked in as I was taking off my coat and hat, and pointed to the note, and the paper, then pointing to her watch, holding up two fingers. Two hours? I asked quietly, and she nodded and went away, after handing me a workbook to record my answers. I sat down, took off my old watch, set it on the table to monitor the time and began to read the questions. I was still writing furiously when she came back and whispered time is up, and held out her hand. I passed her my workbook, and she vanished again, with another smile. It was a strange, lovely, relationship we were developing.

Even though the school term had finished, I kept to my library routine as it helped to fill the days. I enjoyed my time with the librarian, who would often bring in another chair and sit with me in my corner, quietly discussing things I had read about in books, places she had visited. The librarian was well-travelled, and her stories inspired me. Two weeks after my examination, there was a note on my desk - with a cupcake - to say I had passed with distinction. I nearly let out a big "yes!" but remembered just in time where I was.

I danced home that day, high on my success. I wished I had someone with whom to share it. As I reached the farm I nearly stopped, wanting to show father my results, but eventually kept going past, knowing he wouldn't be there, wouldn't care anyway.

Early autumn had been quite manageable. Now, the days were drawing in, and the temperatures dropping fast. When the mountains had their first fall of snow, I knew it wouldn't be long before the forest would be deep in snow also. I realised that once the snow settled, my footprints would be obvious, coming and going to and away from the tree. I began to worry about being found; I worried about staying alive through the winter.

My garden crops were finished. I had to rethink my food strategy. I hoarded my rice, and the few remaining root vegetables. I counted a couple of dozen late apples hanging in a bag in the corner of my room. Once the potatoes were ready in the autumn, I had been digging a sackful at a time and I now had three sacks hanging high outside the tree house to feed me through the winter. I decided that it was time I started trapping.

I took my bucket and the trap from the hooked branch outside the tree house door. I needed to find nuts, and knew there were hickory and beech trees not far from my summer berry patches. I set off at a good pace, watching out for evidence of animals, and keeping as quiet as I could, but I had to rethink my strategy very quickly as I broke clear of the trees. The open area on the lower slopes of the forest had another occupant, one with the same idea as me – collecting nuts for the winter. A big black bear, the same one I had seen making a den, I was sure. She was very efficient at collecting and eating and I hoped that she would leave some for me. She ate a lot, that day. In the late afternoon, she wandered off and carefully avoiding the trees she had foraged from, I filled my bucket with hickory and beechnuts. When I returned to my treehouse, before climbing up, I set the trap in a spot that looked like small animals would pass. I made sure to choose a different location whenever I set the trap, but each time ensured it was always within fifty feet of the big redwood, so I could easily collect the kill. I didn't think that this might not be the best strategy.

After that first day at the house, I hadn't opened any of the cans of food; I figured they would be better left for the cold weather. On one of my forays back at the farm after I had overcome my fear of being caught, I had sneaked into the kitchen where I helped myself to the few remaining preserves that mother had made. They now sat on my pantry ledge, reminding me of her. I wished I had learned how to do preserves when she was alive, and made a note to find a book about it.

I discovered a big section on cookery on my next visit to the library in an area that I'd not explored before. However, when I looked up preserves, I realised I didn't have the right equipment to can, bottle or dry any food. It would have to be a project for another time. I kicked myself, though – if I'd thought about it earlier, I might have been able to get my mother's preserving pan and a few bottles. Although in reality, I was too busy learning everything else. Learning life skills had taken up most of my time that year.

My first effort at trapping, and then skinning a squirrel was successful, and I thanked father for having taught me well. Cooking the squirrel was another matter. Whatever I did, it was awful. Dried out, sinewy - and it stank. I didn't try to cook squirrel again. I kept on trapping, though I disposed of the carcasses well away in another part of the forest, just in case of predators. I made a frame between some branches and anchored to my deck, to stretch and dry the skins, and began to make myself a floor mat. It gave me something else to do.

Soon, I had six good skins, and after trimming each one to a rough square, I made a series of holes around the sides of each skin, using my small awl and the hammer. I carefully threaded string through and around each piece. Joined together they made a great mat for the floor. I calculated that it would take about 56 skins to cover the floor entirely, and had fun that evening working out how long that might take me. About three years, was the answer I got, as I could only dry two skins at a time and each one took a few weeks to completely dry in the warm weather, much longer as the days shortened. At least it was a project to keep me busy and fill in the time.

It was a cold, miserable winter that first year. Christmas came and went, forgotten. Snow lay deep and heavy, and for several weeks in the middle of winter, I found it difficult to go outside for more than a few minutes. It would have been impossible to walk into the village. The days were very short. I got up with the sun and fixed my evening meal in the afternoon before it got too dark. Then, to keep warm, I'd crawl into bed, trying not to use the candles as I had very little wax left.

The most I could do was clamber down the rope ladder each morning with my tin pail of ashes to use the long drop, put a couple of shovels full of snow in the bucket, and fix a load of wood to the pulley. Once back up, I'd winch up the bucket and the wood. I'd use the water for washing – although not much more than my face and hands– and for cooking. I didn't have space to keep more than a couple of day's supply of fuel for the fire on the deck, and no room for extra water either. If I left the filled water bucket outside it froze within a couple of hours. I kept the fire in my little fireplace burning all day, and at night wore all my clothes to bed under the comforter.

I cooked a pot of potatoes each day, and pretty much lived on that, plus the remaining apples in my sack. My nuts were gone. Finally, I got desperate and ate my emergency supply of canned food. The beans one day, the last of the spaghetti the next.

There was a blizzard for three days straight, and the third night the wind howled around the trees so hard even my huge tree shook with its fury. I put the fire out for safety, and climbed into my bed where I just stayed, wrapped in every stitch of clothing I had. It was so cold, I wondered if I'd even make it through the night. The air seemed so thin and the wind sucked at the windows, the door. Would it be possible for the wind to suck up my fort and spin it into the air? That was a fanciful notion, but for a twelve-year-old boy, anything was possible that night.

I began to panic. I had no more food. There was a bucket of water, frozen now since I had put the fire out during the night. What if I died here and no one knew, no one came. Would I just shrivel up, be just a little pile of bones eventually that some wild animal gnawed? Would anyone ever find me? I wondered if the librarian might worry when I didn't turn up, but figured she would put it down to the weather. I was confident she had absolutely no idea where I was living. In the morning, the wind had died down. It seemed very dark still, and when I lifted the curtain, I saw why - snow was half way up the window. It was so cold. I had used up all the wood I had stacked inside, so I couldn't light the fire. How would I get out? If I opened the door, would the snow fall in? I was feeling lightheaded, and very cold. I couldn't recall when I last ate. I pulled the bar away from the door, but didn't try to open it. I lay in my bed, a sense of hopelessness flooding through me. Was this it? The end of my life? Before I had achieved anything?

I must have drifted into a semi-conscious state as I lay there. I recall my mother was with me, and a lot of light and at one point I clearly saw her shaking her head, saying no, this is not the time. I could vaguely hear noises, but didn't connect them to anything. The noises got louder. I was sure someone or something was outside but I was too weak to move from my bed. There was a rap on the window, then again. I was even more terrified now than I had been during the storm. I lifted the sack that covered the window beside me. A face looked in through the glass, and a hand appeared, pointing towards the door. I just looked back, too weak, too scared. I heard the sounds of digging in the snow, and after quite some time the door began to open. I cowered under the covers, believing this was my end.

A wiry Indian man came in. He had a pouch tied at his waist, and he pulled something from it, which he offered to me. I shook my head, but he was insistent and I stretched out my hand, taking something that looked like dried meat. I took a bite, and chewed. Despite my weakness, it tasted good. The man brought wood from the small remaining pile outside, and started the fire. He chopped at the frozen water in the bucket with his knife, and put some in my pot on the fire to melt and heat.

Then he calmly sat on the floor and watched me. I watched him back and that's how we stayed, until the water was warm. The

Indian took something else from his pouch and put it in the water, perhaps some herbs, as the smell was quite pungent. Then he poured some of the water into my cup, and gave it to me. I went to drink it down, the welcome heat overcoming the bitterness of the brew, but he shook his head and took the cup back, indicating I should just sip at the liquid. So I did, until it was gone, and I began to feel less lightheaded. I moved to get out of my bed, and he came over to me, helping me up. I sat on the chair, and he sat back on the floor. Thank you, I said. He smiled, put his hand on my arm.

He stayed with me for some time that day, giving me more of the bitter liquid from time to time. When the skies seemed even greyer, he left, leaving me some nuts, and a little more of the dried meat.

I slept better that night, and woke to a calm day. Late in the morning, a thin, wintry sun rose above the trees. I decided to try to get into the village, to buy food. I needed to bring up more wood, and use the long drop too. I slowly and carefully clambered down the ladder, carrying my shovel. I was still weak, but whatever was in the brew the Indian made had helped me. The man had saved my life. How did he know I was there? Moreover, what had made him climb up to me? Where had he come from and what was his name? I hoped I would see him again, and could thank him properly.

I was wearing all my clothes for warmth, a few of my saved dollars in my pocket. I had to buy candles, too, and I craved some coffee or hot chocolate, something sweet. The snow was packed hard around the base of the tree and my wood hillock had vanished completely.

There was no way I could get anywhere. I couldn't even find the long drop, and just made a hole in the snow by another tree nearby to relieve myself. It took most of the daylight to dig out my woodpile and gather enough to take back up and restart my fire. I ate a little more of the dried meat, and a few of the nuts and drank a cup of warmed water. I was so cold I put my squirrel mat over myself in bed.

A day later, I was even colder, and now ravenously hungry. I decided to make a further attempt to get into the village.

I took the shovel again to use for support and to gauge the depth of the snow as I struggled through the forest. There were trees down, and branches blocked the way I usually walked out, so I diverted to wherever it seemed easiest. I climbed over mounds of snow, with no idea what might be under them or if they would carry my weight. It took way more than an hour just to reach the edge of the forest, where I stashed the shovel for my return. When I got there, I was pleased to see someone had scraped the road clear, no doubt one of the farmers with his plough. The road wasn't widely cleared, just a track one-plough width but that was plenty good enough to walk along, although it was slow going. The snow banks were maybe five feet each side. I realised how tall I had grown as I could see clear across the top of the banked snow to the farms as I walked past.

By the time I got to the village, I was hot and tired, despite the freezing temperatures, and I worried again about being seen and recognised. I looked around me, to see if there was anyone I might know. There was not a soul to be seen thank goodness, and I quickly ducked into the general store. It was the first time I had been in there since I left the farm. I kept my hat on, and my head down as I picked up candles, matches, coffee and hot chocolate, sugar, some canned goods. More potatoes, onion, carrots. I took everything to the counter. I had been practising what I would say to the grocer when he asked me where I'd been, what I had been doing. When I reached the counter, I was surprised. I didn't recognise the woman who served me at all. I guess my demeanour was such that she picked I wasn't the talking type, and merely told me the cost. I paid over most of my dollars and put my purchases in my old bag; turned and moved out of the store as quickly as I could. I wondered who she was, and what had happened to the grocer who had run the store as long as I could remember. I reminded myself to ask the librarian.

The library was across the road and down a little. As I walked from the store, I recognised two of my old classmates wheeling a handcart along, loaded with a heavy-looking package. I guessed the school must have closed because of the weather. Behind them, the doctor stood chatting to the publican. I put my head down, pulled my hat well forward and walked swiftly in the opposite direction. I turned the corner of the block and kept going, past the back of the library building. I sidled up and peered around the corner back to the main street. It seemed clear now, and I hurried along as fast as I could without attracting attention. Unfortunately, I was so busy keeping my head down that I didn't see the doctor turn into the library ahead of me, and stand by the door. I bumped right into him, dropping my bag on the ground. Cans and potatoes rolled around the entrance, and I scrambled to retrieve them. Hello my boy, said the doctor. Good to see you. He patted my head. I stood up, afraid, He must have seen the look on my face, as he smiled kindly, and went on his way. Not a word about where I had been, what I was doing, nothing. I was puzzled, but relieved.

I slid through the doorway and went straight into my corner, removed my outer garments and my thick boots and sat at my desk. Whew, I thought that was difficult. The doctor knows I'm here, now. I was going to have to figure out another way of getting to the store, and to the library. I was lucky it was still so cold out that most folk had stayed indoors today.

It was only a few minutes until the librarian put her head around the screen, bringing me coffee and a big piece of apple pie. I'm pretty sure the rules about no food or drink in the library hadn't changed, but I wasn't turning any food down, that's for sure. Especially not when the librarian herself brought it to me. I ate and drank gratefully. That was the best pie I had ever tasted and the coffee, hot and sweet and milky, warmed me right through.

I said I had seen the doctor. She shrugged, and then said she didn't think that was a problem. She told me when I asked that the previous owner of the general store had moved on. His wife had left with a trapper in the autumn of the previous year, and the grocer decided to chance his luck in a city. The new owners seemed quite nice, but kept to themselves. They had two small children. She was letting me know, without directly saying, that it would be safe to go into the general store for provisions, as they wouldn't know my situation. I was beginning to think the librarian knew everything that was happening in the town. Of course, now I know that she would have been well aware of the dynamics of the entire community. However, at the end of the day she came back with a key for the back entrance, and suggested I enter the library that way, as I was less likely to meet up with anyone. Even better, she brought me more food, a beef pie this time. I tried to eat it slowly, but I'm afraid it disappeared like a rabbit in a magician's hat. The librarian laughed as I devoured the pie.

On the way home that night the snow started again. Within half an hour, my face was so chilled my teeth rattled, and it hurt to breathe. I pulled my scarf across my nose and mouth and hurried as fast as I could. I knew my way well, but still it was very slow getting home. After reaching the forest, I made a couple of wrong turnings before I reached my tree, and kept stumbling over the submerged and fallen branches scattered around. I filled my bucket with snow, collected a load of wood in my ashes pail, and climbed the rope ladder. It was a relief to be inside and out of the weather, and I forgot to check my trap, which had become part of my usual afternoon routine. After emptying my bag of shopping, I lit my little fire, and put snow into the pot to make myself a warm coffee. I really missed milk, but the sugar I had bought made the drink sweet and the fire made it smoky. It was great. I sat on my bed, feeling the warmth trickle down my throat, into my stomach.

It seemed easier to manage everything, that night. Whether it was the coffee, some food, the walk into the village, I didn't know. There was a feeling that things were not as bad as I thought and I could survive the winter in my little house. During the night, I heard my mother, singing softly; her tune one I had heard often as a child. For a moment, I could faintly hear the sound of a rocking chair – the one in the kitchen at the farm; it had a particular tiny squeak on the forward rock. I went to sleep to the sound, comforted.

The snowfall this time lasted only through that night and the next day. When I went out the following day, I checked my trap and found a rabbit, my first one. The carcass had frozen solid, in the trap, and it took me some time to remove it. In the end, I had to break its leg. First I apologised to the rabbit for what I was about to do, then gave a quick wrench. The crack sounded so loud in the silent, snow-filled forest. I pulled the body out and then reset the trap.

Once thawed, skinned and gutted, I put the rabbit in the pot to cook the way I had seen mother do it, with onions and potato and my last carrot. I didn't have any herbs, but put in some of the dried-up blueberries. It simmered all day, and the smell wafted about and filled my little house. When I finally decided it was ready, it was the best rabbit I'd ever eaten and I slept well with a full stomach.

I had totally forgotten about wild animals picking up on the scent, mainly because I hadn't seen any so far that winter. The next morning I woke to find my tree shaking. It wasn't the same way it had shaken in the storm. This was quite a different movement, and a lot more scary. I wondered what it was, and then realised I might be in trouble when I heard sniffling, scrabbling noises outside. I quietly, carefully went over to the door and opened it just a fraction. I couldn't see anything, but there was definitely something down there. I leaned over the edge.

The biggest black bear ever. About ten feet up the tree. Heading my way. I froze, and fortunately, he didn't see me. He sniffed about, scraped at the bark, and then dropped back down to the ground. I watched the bear walk around the base of the tree. He stood up again and stretched against the tree, his paws clawing at the bark. He must have smelled the rabbit and thought he'd invite himself over for a meal. The bear must have been fully-grown or close to it, because from where I was, he appeared to be six or seven feet tall and weighed maybe 500 pounds or more. I had thought they hibernated all winter, so perhaps this chap had a bad nightmare or maybe he just woke up and felt like a snack. I tried to remember everything I had read at the library about bears. Nothing except the fact that black bears are excellent trees climbers came to mind. I was so frightened I could hardly breathe. I got a cramp in my leg but was afraid to move even a fraction to straighten it, or try to shift from my ledge, in case he saw the movement or heard me moving. So there I sat, half in the door, half on the ledge, silently willing the knot in my leg and the accompanying pain to disappear. I remembered the book said bears attack if hungry. How hungry was he? Would he be very hungry? How far could he climb? Should I throw down the rest of the rabbit – or would that encourage him to come looking for more? He had clearly picked up a scent but seemed a bit confused. The bear went over to where I set had my trap and banged at it with his paw. I saw what he had found – another rabbit. I guess he didn't expect a rabbit to be up a tree. He tried to push off the trap, and then bit into the rabbit, whacking at the trap to dislodge it. Man, one bear hit and the trap sailed off into the undergrowth. Maybe he ought to play baseball I thought to myself. I tried to pinpoint in my mind where the trap went as it disappeared. The rabbit eaten, I watched as the bear returned to my tree, and start sniffing again.

This time he began to climb. I was terrified. I crawled back into my house, hoping that his climbing would stop him noticing any other movement. I shut the door carefully, and secured it with the wooden bar. I checked I had shut the windows tight, and pulled the sacking blinds down over the panes. I sat down with my back against the door, bracing myself, getting more scared every minute. I could feel the tree shaking as the bear climbed and the noise he made was getting louder and louder. I felt him pause when he reached the tree house and start sniffing around. I held my breath. He could smell my rabbit stew, I was sure. He banged the metal chimney, but stopped when he burnt his paw and let out a roar. I sat motionless against the door, terrified he would smash the window and put in his paw to grab me. One swipe and I'd either be bear breakfast, or make a record for the highest a boy had ever been thrown from a tree. The ledge creaked and groaned with the bear's weight. He headed up one branch, past the house then came back down. He whacked a paw against the roof and I felt it give a bit in the corner. For a moment, I thought he was going to actually climb up and stand on the roof and I didn't think the structure I had built would stand up to that much weight. He might make me into a sandwich filling between the roof and the floor, squashing me to death, and no one would ever find the remains. He leaned against the house and I saw it move. I almost stopped breathing then. He sat there, outside, leaning against the house having a look about. I sat there, inside, cowering up against the door. It seemed hours before he shifted his weight off the side and I felt him move to the edge of the deck, but in reality, it was probably only a few minutes. I didn't dare move even to look at my watch, which I usually kept hanging on a hook beside my bed. I heard thumping, ripping and cracking noises, and the tree shook. I couldn't figure out what he was doing but I knew it wasn't anything good. Finally, it appeared that he was moving away and then it seemed he had commenced his descent.

I waited and waited until long after the tree stopped shaking. I was still shaking, however. Once I was confident that I couldn't hear any noises at all, I carefully lifted the bar off the door, trying not to make a sound. I opened the door and went out. I peered down. No bear that side. I sidled my way around the miniscule decking, across the tree branches and looked all around the tree. Nope, no bear. There were big claw marks everywhere and he'd made a real mess of the chimney. It hung loose and I was concerned about the possibility of a fire. The bear had torn my small wood box off the branch and it now lay in pieces way down on the ground. He had destroyed the frame I had made for stretching skins and the skin that had been on it was now ripped and chewed. The side of the house where the bear had sat himself down was pushed on an angle, and one branch had a huge crack in it. I was thankful the bear hadn't picked a branch that supported the tree house to use as his lookout post.

I went back inside. I stayed there all day. I let the fire go out, so the chimney would cool and I could repair it. I didn't cook that day; I ate my leftover rabbit cold. I kept shaking. I thought I'd not trap any more this winter, so the bear wouldn't come back. If he knew there would be meat waiting in the trap, he'd keep turning up, I reasoned. I was concerned the smell of my rabbit cooking would encourage him to pay another uninvited visit at mealtime.

However, if I couldn't fix the chimney, I wouldn't be cooking anything. That night I went to bed cold, but not hungry, thanks to the rabbit leftovers. I ventured out in the morning to find the trap where the bear had thrown it. After some time I located it, quite a way from my tree, caught up on a branch in the undergrowth. While it was a bit battered and bent, it was still usable. I put the trap in my bag, got more wood and water, used the long drop and clambered back up my ladder, noting the bear claw marks all the way. I fixed the trap, before turning my attention to the chimney. There was a huge gash in the metal, from where it came out of the wall of the house right up to where I had anchored it by the edge of the roof. Somehow, I had to repair the cut, then re-fix the pipe to the wall and back into the firebox. I looked in the small toolbox I had brought, seeking rivets, or a spare strip of metal, but no luck. I cursed aloud, grateful for once that my whisperer wasn't around to hear me and scold. I was going to have to go back to the farm, and find what I could there. And in this weather, it was unlikely father would have made his way to the bar – more likely he'd had the publican deliver his whisky to the farm. Unless he still had supplies in the cellar.

I was still worried about the bear paying me another visit, too. If he was hungry, he'd go to a known food source – me. What if the bear was lurking somewhere near my tree, waiting for me? But I didn't have a choice, I had to fix the chimney or I'd freeze to death.

With a sigh, I secured my house, and with a hammer and tin snips in my coat pocket trudged through the deep snow, clambering around and over the fallen trees and branches – now almost hidden under the latest snow falls – and out to the road. I did my usual sweep from left to right searching the area. No one in sight. The banks of snow provided good cover although they made progress slow. I skirted the edge of the trees carefully, and crept, keeping as low as I could, across the neighbour's farm. I crawled through the first fence, over the second and around to the back of father's barn. Granddad had always kept the workbench neat and tidy, and I had learned from him to do the same. I had assumed I would find something suitable with little effort and be able to return the way I had come quite quickly. But the workbench and the ground around it were all in a total mess. Tools thrown down carelessly and nails spilled everywhere. Material lying haphazardly around. I guessed father had been looking for something or trying to repair something. I suspected animals might have been in there as well, from the smell. I started to rummage through an old pile of metal in one corner, looking for a piece of a flat sheet that might fit, and was so focused in my search I almost missed the sound of voices and heavy boots crunching across the snow. Just in time, I ducked down and pulled my hat low.

The farmer from across the road strode in, looking around him as he did. Father limped in after him, dragging his left leg. I wondered what was wrong with it. Then I thought - had they seen my footprints? I tried to breathe as quietly as possible. My heart was beating fast. The two men went over to the tractor and tried to start it. The engine turned over, coughed, stopped. Father walked across to the workbench, searching for a tool. He picked up a wrench, looking over towards the corner I was hiding in as he returned to the tractor. I willed myself not to move. Had he seen me? I didn't think so. Father stopped, and I noticed the expression on his face – he had an idea something wasn't quite right, but couldn't pin it down. He shrugged and turned back to the tractor. The neighbour had already lifted the cover to expose the engine and the two men worked at the repair, scarcely speaking. How's your boy? The neighbour asked. Took hisself off to live with my sister, father said. Haven't heard from him since. Hmm, said the neighbour noncommittally. He's a good boy. Did a man's job helping me last summer cleaning out the barn. Pity he's not around. I'd be keen to have a boy like that working for me again. Can't do it all on my own. How you managing here, anyhows? Bah said father. I've no interest in it now Rose has gone. The boy isn't much to worry about he added, seemingly as an afterthought.

After that, Father didn't say another word for quite some time as they worked on the tractor, tested it, revved it up and eventually decided they had fixed the problem.

I heard my father thank the neighbour as they walked outside. No problem, neighbours need to help each other out up here, he replied. Pity about your boy being gone.

And then he raised his voice a little, turned slightly back towards the barn, towards me, and said, well, if he comes back, tell him to call over to me come summer and I'll fix him up some work. Pay proper, too. And meals. He'll be needing some money in his pocket I expect.

He knew I was there, I was sure. I waited and waited until I heard nothing before getting up. My legs had gone stiff, crouched up in the corner. I resumed my search, but warily, keeping an ear out for any noise that might herald the return of my father to the barn. I found a piece of downpipe which I thought might work better than my riveting a piece of metal over the gash and would certainly be easier to join. After searching around the junk pile a bit more I found some gasket tar to use as a sealant, and put that in my pocket.

When I was sure no one was near, I returned the way I had come. The cold weather had iced the ground, freezing my footprints and they were very noticeable. There was no way the neighbour would have missed them. Maybe he thought they had been father's, I tried to rationalise, but then it dawned on me they were only going one way. I tried to step in them, sliding my foot about to confuse anyone who might see the footprints into thinking someone had gone out of the barn, rather than into it, as I hurried back to the forest, but it was obvious really and I was thankful not to see anyone. The more I thought about it the more I was sure the neighbour knew I was in the barn. I was positive he aimed his sentence directly at me. Now yet another person knew I was still around and hadn't gone to Aunt Sally's, I thought.

It took the rest of the day to finish all the repairs, and then I had to restart the fire to check the chimney was working effectively. The wood box had to be completely rebuilt, and so did the stretching frame, but the latter was going to have to wait a few days to be attended to. I boiled a little water and made myself a warm drink, then had a second cold meal, being a bit nervous about cooking anything, or even heating up the remaining scraps of rabbit in a pot in case the scent tempted that bear back. The new piece of pipe worked even better than the first, or maybe the sealant had provided a better join than my earlier efforts. Either way, the chimney drew well, and by dark, I settled myself inside again.

Dreams about the bear ripping my house then attacking me woke me twice in the night, and then I lay awake, sweating, despite the cold of the room as the fire had gone out, and worried that the farmer or the doctor would tell others I was around. Not much I could do about the bear – or any telling either. I got up and restarted the fire, pulling in the last of the wood off the deck. I made myself another warm drink of chocolate and finally went back to sleep just as the light started to filter through the trees.

The days passed. I wrote in my book about the Indian who saved my life, the bear and the visit to the barn. I drew some sketches of ideas for houses, and read a book I'd brought home from the library. The menu after the rabbit stew was finished was mostly potatoes again with an occasional can of food. I began to feel cabin fever coming on and was desperate to get outside – but apart from my usual routine, I didn't feel safe about venturing far from the tree in case the bear returned.

I think I made the right decision. The bear was back a week or so later. I was sure it was the same one – small head, pale snout, a white mark on its back – sniffing around the trap. The trap was empty. I hadn't tried to catch anything – I hadn't even set the trap. After batting the trap about the forest floor for a short while, the bear sniffed around the woodpile and the place where I had dug my toilet. This time he didn't seem interested in climbing the tree and after stomping around the clear space at the base of the tree, and sharpening his claws on the bark, he wandered off. Shortly after, I heard something crashing through the undergrowth, and a deer darted through, followed by the bear. I wondered if the deer had escaped safely, and hoped so.

After the second visit by the bear, I waited several days before I reset the trap. I moved it to a new location each time, but still kept it not far off the path that took me to the road. I wanted some more squirrel skins for my floor mat to make the place a bit warmer – and on the very cold nights, the squirrel mat had become a welcome extra cover. I was careful to take myself off to different spots in the forest far from my tree before I skinned the animals. It was impossible to dig any holes in the frozen ground so I carefully buried the remains under piles of rocks. I hoped that any smells would divert the bear, or any other wild animal, well away from the tree and me.

By the end of the winter, I had a mat made of 18 skins, mostly squirrel, apart from three pelts that were rabbit. It looked a little odd, but certainly made the floor – and me - warmer. From time to time, I heard bears below me, but none climbed the tree again that year.

The Indian did though. Several times over that winter he would climb my tree and visit. He didn't need the rope ladder, which amazed me. We found a way to converse, and twice I cooked a meal for him. I had asked him how he found me, and he said he had watched me since I was young, building the tree house. He was interested by my building, and keen to know what I was going to do when I had completed the structure. When I had moved into the house he was astonished – a little kid in the forest – and he decided to watch out for me. He said he was concerned when the blizzard came, and felt he had to come and check that I was all right. He took me on trips through the forest, showing me plants I could eat, nuts that were safe. He indicated that the bear was now back in hibernation, so cooking rabbit would not put me at risk. He helped me with my trap, and brought me a skin one day that was as soft as velvet. I asked him if he would show me how to cure my rabbit skins the way this one was, and he spent time teaching me. Though he was somewhat older than me, we grew to be good friends and I treasured the times we had together.

Chapter Six: Friends and Secrets

The melt was early in the spring, as if to atone for the bitter winter. Now that it was easier to get through the snow in the forest, I resumed my regular journey to the library, just three days a week at first and then back to four. It gave me some contact with society, and I had missed my interaction with the librarian. She was my only link to the outside world, and as such I depended upon her a lot. My desire to learn was like a dry sponge finding a deep bowl of water, and to me the library provided a bottomless vessel of information and enlightenment.

The space in the corner of the library had become my daytime refuge. I was clear in my intention to become an architect. How I would achieve this goal wasn't so clear. But studying hard, and keeping focused were the things I could do, so that's what I did. Like that first day in the forest, when my mother came and helped me write the answers in my book, I knew that I was taking the right path, and the solutions would come.

In late April, I was out looking for bait for my trap, not far from where the mother bear had made her den. She emerged, two cubs with her and they wandered off together to forage. There was plenty of spring grass around, and I spent a long time observing them from a distance, as they feasted on the green shoots sprouting on the trees, and the fallen nuts. The mother bear waded into the stream, snatching up little fish and munching on them, the cubs copying her movements.

One morning, as I walked past along the road, the farmer who had been so kind to me before I left home was standing beside his mailbox. I tried to hurry past but he called out to me and I couldn't pretend I hadn't seen him, didn't know him. Putting his hand on my shoulder, he looked at me and smiled. You good boy? I nodded, but kept my head lowered. Had the other neighbour told him I was around? What if he said I had to go with him, or go back home, or something? He took his hand off my shoulder and tipped his hat back. You take care of yourself he said. I'll have the wife put a basket on the mailbox for you from time to time, so look out for it. I nodded again, and moved on. I knew he stood and watched me for quite some time as I continued down the road. I was still so scared that someone would make me go back to father at the farm. That afternoon, on my way back to the forest, I went a circuitous route, which added about two more miles to the journey. It was almost dark when I got back to my tree house, and I was tired. I decided that I'd either have to chance meeting someone, or leave earlier in both the morning and afternoon if I intended to take the longer route. I tossed one of my remaining coins. Heads long route, tails shorter route. It fell on the floor tails up.

The next morning I set out again. As I neared the neighbour's I looked around carefully and furtively to check for anyone. I couldn't see a soul, and I felt heartened. As I drew level with their mailbox, however, I noticed a basket sitting on the top. I looked up the track to their farmhouse, where a lace curtain twitched at a window, and a hand waved. I went over to the basket and peeked in. The neighbour's wife had prepared me a feast. Something warm that smelled wonderful in a parcel wrapped with a cloth and well tied up with string, a plate with cake, and a small cookie box. I lifted down the basket, waved back, and carried it as I continued on my way into the village.

At midday, I went around to a spot near the back entrance of the library where there was an old metal seat. I brushed the snow off and sat down to feast on my basket of food. The cloth-wrapped parcel contained a lidded tin dish filled with beef stew. There was cherry cake, raisin cookies. It all tasted wonderful, and I made it last as long as I could. Everything seemed brighter after that meal, and I felt a sense of not being so alone. I counted up the adults who knew I was still living somewhere around the village. Two neighbours, the doctor, the librarian. I guess the schoolmaster did too, otherwise how would the librarian have obtained my work assignments and examinations? I decided that if they knew about me and hadn't done anything about it already, then they weren't likely to. The woman at the store had seen me once, but she didn't know me at all, so wouldn't be aware that I was supposed to be somewhere else.

I resumed my routine of schoolwork and pleasure reading. I had returned the empty basket to the mailbox on my way home that first day with a note to say thank you, and every day there would be another one waiting for me in the mornings. It made my existence so much easier. I came in the same days each week so the farmer's wife knew when she could safely leave the basket for me to pick up. The basket of food I was given became my only meal on days I went into the village. I kept on making my stews, most times I caught a rabbit. They were mostly just rabbit and water with just a little rice or potato now, as my supplies were dwindling fast. I was able to leave a rabbit or two in the mailbox some mornings when I collected my meal basket and I felt that I was making some recompense for all their kindnesses. I made a second trip to the store one day, and used the last of my coins on more rice and several cans of black chilli beans. If the woman in the general store wondered where I was from, she never asked, just gave me my purchases with a smile. My rabbit stew with beans was pretty good, I thought.

In early summer, the librarian set me my next round of examinations. Mathematics, science, English, calculus, classics. Again, I did well, and I was proud of my efforts. I hoped that somehow my mother knew that I was succeeding and that her whispers had proved correct so far.

When school was over for the summer, I decided to take up the suggestion casually made by the farmer who had helped father with the tractor. I walked to his farmhouse early one morning and went round to the back door. He must have seen me coming – or perhaps his wife did, and called to him – for he was standing by the door, waiting. He held out his hand to shake mine, with a smile on his face. I asked if he might have any work for me, not letting on that I had seen him in the barn with father, and he said he was so pleased I'd come. He had work right through the summer for me if I wanted it. Good pay, a new pair of boots, and all my meals. Both the boots and the meals were a godsend.

So early each day, except for Sundays, I would bathe in the stream and then walk to work. Breakfast would be waiting for me, bacon and eggs, hash browns, sausage. We'd stop for lunch, thick sandwiches with cheese and pickles that the farmer's wife brought outside to us. As the sun slowed we'd wash up and enter the house to eat an evening meal, then I would say goodnight and return to the tree house. After doing my own few chores, I'd fall asleep, tired but content.

I hoed and harrowed, cleaned out the wintering barn again, planted, helped with the grain harvest, pruned the orchard, all the usual farm work. The farmer asked if I'd work his vegetable garden, and gave me a corner to plant for myself, as well. I bought my own seeds from the general store, and seed potatoes as well. It was a good long hot summer and everything thrived. For fun, I also planted cornflowers and the pretty blue reminded me of mother. I took to cutting a few and keeping them in an old jar with water in my tree house.

The farmer never asked where I lived, not once. His wife mothered me. She taught me how to make pancakes. She brought me a pair of sturdy tweed trousers one day, and made me take off my old ripped and shrunken pair. They were scarcely decent, she said. And another time she gave me two new shirts, and a used, but still serviceable overcoat. For your birthday, she said with a smile. I had completely forgotten my birthday in the early spring, several months before. I suddenly realised I was now thirteen.

I saved most of my wages to add to my college fund. I bought plenty of dried and canned goods to last the coming winter, two new warm blankets, extra candles, matches, and other provisions, along with two new pails to carry it all. Several new notebooks to write in, pencils. My house was stuffed full of provisions and things to make life more comfortable this year.

On my day off each week, I worked around the tree house, making it stronger, sturdier. I built a much better safe in the branches to store vegetables and to hang any animals, replacing the one I had roughly created after the bear had wrecked the first one. I figured that if another bear came, he would attack the safe first. I cut loads more wood, so I would not run out over winter, and created a wood bin with a hinged lid off the end of the decking by building out and around between two branches. It gave me a place to store a lot more wood, which meant I didn't have to winch up wood each day as before. The two extra pails enabled me to store more water, and I felt a little safer – I could douse the fire quickly if needed. In addition, I put in some more shelving. I made a frame for my bed, both to make it longer, and to raise it off the floor. I was a bit short of padding, and my feet rested on bare wood, but at least they didn't still hang over the edge. It also gave me space to store things underneath – sorely needed now I had collected up so much more.

My Indian friend and I went for walks in my forest. It had become my home and much of it was now familiar, more so as he pointed out places, taught me things. I picked a pail of blueberries one day for the farmer's wife as a gift, and a few days later, there were two jars of blueberry jam beside my plate at breakfast, for me to take away. I shared one jar with my new friend, making him my rice and blueberry mush. He liked it as much as I did. I felt a lot more confident and capable now. I had managed one whole year. I had grown taller and stronger, and I knew a lot more about looking after myself.

I had planted mostly autumn crops in the space the farmer let me use – root vegetables that would last in the winter: carrots, turnips, swede, potato, sweet potato – and greens such as cabbage that kept well. As the vegetables grew to maturity, I pulled them and put them in my safe in the tree.

One morning the farmer took me across to father's farm, to shear our old sheep. I was a bit concerned and rather reluctant to go, until he looked at me and said, he won't recognise you, boy, don't worry. He probably won't come out of the house even if he is here. And he was right, father never appeared. After the shearing, I grabbed some of the wool, stuffed it into a new bale the famer had given me, and hauled it on my sled back to the forest, where I used it to pack out my new bed. It was almost luxurious.

My Indian friend was impressed with my bed. He lay on it, laughing, calling me – or the bed – a "softy"; well, I think that was what he meant. He would arrive, without notice, and sit on the bed, helping me soften my rabbit skins and talking, or taking me off to see things in the forest.

At the end of the summer, my work was pretty much finished. The farmer could manage the remaining farm chores, and it was time for me to restart my studies. His wife gave me a big basket, full of preserves, and some cheeses. My college fund was growing. I had plenty of food to last the coming winter. The very best gift, the one most important, was that they had accepted me and kept my secret and I was truly grateful.

I took the basket home and arranged the preserves on my shelves. The cheeses I hung in the corner beside my apples. My house had become a real home.

From time to time, I'd see my other neighbour, whose wife had made me baskets all winter. He'd wave, and I'd wave back. Of course, they knew I was working across the road – I know now that the two farmers and their wives had worked out between them how to care for me in a way I would accept. I think they also looked after my father, although nothing was ever said, and I never asked.

The second winter would be easier, I thought. I could manage better, as I knew what to expect. I had more provisions, and was much better prepared.

I had resumed my trips to the library and started on my schooling. The librarian came in to talk with me from time to time, and I told her about my summer job, my Indian friend. She brought me new books to study, detailed books on architecture. I devoured them after I finished the work I had assigned myself each day.

I kept foraging on my days away from the library. In many places, fallen trees from the previous year's storm covered the tracks I had used before, and I had to create new paths to get to the berry patches. I carefully looked for animal droppings, to gauge their feeding places, and to make sure I wasn't in their line of sight or smell. I came across the mother bear again – this time making her den under a tree that had fallen on an angle into the undergrowth, leaving a good bear-size space. I skirted the tree, and was extra careful to stay away from the area. I wondered why she had not returned to the cave she had so carefully dug out the previous year, until on another of my excursions I saw that another bear had claimed it.

Once the weather closed in again the mailbox baskets reappeared as if by magic. With a bigger bed and more bedding, and more food – as well as being more proficient with cooking on the tiny fireplace, I was content. I hadn't heard my mother for a while, and began to think that maybe she had moved on. I missed her.

While the weather this winter was less ferocious, it stayed cold and snowy for longer and my birthday passed again. It fell on a Saturday and I was now fourteen. I did remember this year, and on the way home from the library the day before had bought some eggs and milk at the general store. I made pancakes the way the farmer's wife had taught me, and opened the other jar of blueberry jam. Spread between layers of pancake, my meal tasted of summer and happy times and that night my mother was back, whispering happy birthday my boy.

The squeak of the rocking chair, that seemed so real, lulled me to sleep.

The next school day my mailbox basket seemed to weigh a lot heavier than normal. Snow was falling lightly, so I waited till I had reached the library and settled myself before removing the cover. Inside I found a cake and a note saying happy birthday as well as my meal; and a parcel addressed to me from my Aunt Sally. I wondered how the neighbours had that, and decided even the mailman must be part of the secret. Aunt Sally had sent me a new sweater, red, with a rolled collar. I shared the cake with the librarian and showed her my gift. She suggested I write back straight away to my aunt to thank her, and I took her wise counsel, mailing the letter from the post box at the general store. I mentioned in the letter that father and I were somewhat estranged, and that sending any mail in the future to the farm next door would be a better option. I knew she would understand.

March and April sped by, and in May I took my examinations. I had studied hard over the winter and spring. I wanted to get the best grades I could, so that when I applied to a university at the end of the following year I would possibly be eligible for a scholarship. For three weeks, I waited on tenterhooks and when the results finally arrived, I was too nervous to open the envelope myself. I handed it back to the librarian, who slit the top neatly with her paper knife and withdrew the contents. I watched her reading the single sheet, and a huge smile lit her face as she told me I had scored the highest marks in the state.

Chapter Seven: Learning Growing Understanding

It was now three years since I'd left the farm. I had myself a life, with a routine. While it didn't seem that exciting, it was what I had created for myself. The winter had passed without incident – or rather, I managed the incidents better. I had learned what to do to ensure the winter was manageable and my little tree house was quite cosy with the wool insulated walls and the improved fireplace. I saw several bears as I was out foraging, but none climbed my tree again, at least not when I was around. I figured I ought to thank the bear that had climbed, as he taught me to be more aware of the environment, gave me ideas for improving the tree house, and showed me I had strength enough to live in the forest safely.

I admit the baskets of food left for me on the mailbox were a godsend and I found it hard to express my thanks in ways other than a note or a rabbit from time to time. It made my life so much easier, not having to cook so much at night. It seemed that as I grew, the contents of the baskets did too.

I now had to duck my head to get through the door of my tree house, and the tree house seemed far smaller than when it first became my home. Climbing up to my home was almost effortless and took much less time. Inside I could still stand straight, but less comfortably. Once again my feet hung over the end of my bed, but there was little I could do to change that – if I lengthened the bed, I would not be able to open or close the door, and that wasn't an option. Creating and designing structures consumed me. I thought about making changes to my tree house, extending walls, making a bigger space for sleeping. That summer I asked the farmer if I could work only five days each week, and said that I wanted to study more. We talked a lot as we worked together on the farm – about all sorts of things. Like building, and what was happening in cities, and life in general. One day he surprised me with a book on designs for farmhouses that he had sent away for from a catalogue and we pored over it, looking at the drawings. That book was instrumental in confirming my plans for my future. He was keen to build a new farmhouse, and was very interested in my ideas, especially ways for keeping houses warmer. One day I let slip that I lived in the forest. Of course, he said, we always knew that, and went back to what he had been discussing. I told him that once I had my qualification I would come back and design better houses and barns that met the needs of the farming community, and I could build them, too. He thought that a wonderful plan.

How I could have imagined they didn't know I lived in the forest, I don't know. I guess I was just a kid, absorbed by what I was doing, not aware of what went on around me.

Over that summer, I put my reading, studying and increased knowledge to practical use. I put up shelving and new cupboards for the farmer's wife in her kitchen, repaired their chimney and the roof, and did all manner of tasks to improve their farmhouse in addition to my work in the fields and the garden.

I worked hard on my days off making the tree house larger. I was used to ducking as I went in and out and chose to leave the door the size it was. I had figured out a way to increase the space by building around the huge branches and cantilevering over the trunk. I extended the tiny ledge I had called a deck, as it had become far too small for me to manoeuvre safely around the outside of the house. Inside, I had a branch coming in through one wall and out another, which looked odd but worked fine, and the extra space enabled me to add a further fourteen inches to the length of the bed. This meant that I had to turn myself around for sleeping, putting my head at the door end, and my feet into the extension underneath the tree branch. I made myself a little headboard beside the door and it all worked fine. Of course, I then needed a longer mattress – again.

That year's wool clip once again provided what I needed. Father's ram had died during the winter and although there were a few new lambs, it was evident when the farmer and I went over to shear them that the ewes were in poor condition. The wool was barely usable, so filled with dirt and tangles. The farmer mentioned how run-down the farm was becoming. I felt a great level of guilt. If I had stayed at the farm, I could have looked after the stock better. I could have fixed up the farmhouse and maybe father would have stopped drinking and become happier. When I suggested all this to the farmer's wife one day, she looked at me in amazement. You did what you needed to do, she said. It was your father's role to protect you, not the other way around. He didn't do that. You are not to feel guilty, or take on that responsibility. Still, I felt it inside.

I had become quite proficient at cooking for myself. My foraging in the forest that year netted me pounds and pounds of blueberries and strawberries, and I took my pails full of sweet fruit into the farmer's wife. She taught me how to make preserves with the berries, and with the apples and pears I filched from my old home across the road when I knew father wasn't there. Together we sent away for books about cooking and herbs, and we grew a wonderful vegetable garden. Even the farmer said the meals had improved.

My trapping improved too, and I now put out several traps. My floor mat finally grew to the 56 skins I had calculated when I first started out – a good mix of squirrel and rabbit. It seemed a lifetime ago that I had figured out that mat, far longer than a couple of years. The extensions I made to the room that summer resulted in the mat being a little short of covering the entire floor, but it was perfectly adequate. I trapped as often as I could, now that I knew how to cure skins till they were soft and velvety, and with the assistance from my friend in doing it, it didn't take long for me to have sufficient rabbit pelts to make myself a wonderfully warm and cosy cover for my "softy" bed as well. I learned how to sew them – as the squaws did, my friend said – using a bone hook and fine sinew.

Some days I would take a skinned rabbit or two with me when I went to work for the farmer's wife to make one of her wonderful rich stews, and as a way to thank them both for their kindness to me.

The extra space in the tree house enabled me to extend the shelving, and I put my preserves proudly on display. I now had enough room to shelve all the new books I had accumulated, including my several notebooks full of writing and drawings. The writing was mostly about my day, as I had vowed to myself when I started out; the drawings were ideas for buildings, fixing things, making houses better and more functional. I wrote out how to cure the rabbit skins, the way my Indian friend had shown me; how to make a bone needle and sinew thread, how to sew the skins together. How I cooked my meals. Foods that could be found in the forest, and things that were not safe to consume. I carefully documented the building process of the tree house, with illustrations, in a separate notebook and I had dreams of one day turning it into a real book.

On my way home to the forest after work one evening, lost in thought and not heeding the road particularly, I walked past an old man, drunk and unsteady, stumbling along, leg dragging. He tripped over and fell down, face in the gravel. My first thought was to move on quickly, but then something made me stop and turn back. I was hesitant to involve myself, but I helped the man up, realising with shock that it was my father. He didn't appear to recognise me. His clothes were ragged and dirty, his hair a mess.

I nearly turned and walked away, nearly didn't speak to him, after he was standing again. I wasn't that scared, hurt boy who left all those years ago. I wasn't afraid that he might hit me –

indeed, I was far taller and stronger now. I felt numb. I felt as if he was someone I might have once met years ago.

Nevertheless, he was my father, and he was unwell. His leg dragged even more than when I had noticed it that day in the barn. I pretended I didn't know him, and asked where he lived, and he pointed in the direction of the farmhouse. I asked him about his leg. He said his doctor thought he might have had a stroke. I took his weight as we moved slowly along. His clothes and body smelled. His breath was foul. This was my father. What was left of him. This is what we had come to, a man and his son, grown, unknowing of each other's life. When we reached his mailbox, he said he could go the rest of the way on his own. I offered to keep walking with him, but he said no, he could manage the distance. He shook my hand and thanked me. His handshake was surprisingly firm.

I stood and watched him shamble his way down the drive to the farmhouse, open the kitchen door and disappear inside. Did he recognise me? I will never know.

I tried to remember the good times, my mother and he laughing, happy. I looked around me for that little boy who was safe and protected by his loving family. I couldn't see him. My heart ached. For us all, for what had happened and how our lives had become. I walked slowly along the road, and into the forest, until I reached my tree. That night, I sat in the tree house and looked at the photograph of mother. In my heart, I knew that was the last time I would talk to my father. Something shifted that night. The black knot of anger that I had carried around inside me started to dissolve. I felt lighter, less tense. I had started to forgive him. I began to forgive myself. I grew up a lot that night. The shift from thinking as a boy to reasoning as a adult had begun and I wasn't surprised that my mother was hovering around the edges of my dreams as I slept. She held a tape measure, was measuring something, marking something on the tape, not far from the end. I couldn't quite see what it was, although I could sense she was trying to tell me something important.

I spent a lot of time thinking as I walked the road each workday, and at night, cocooned in my tree house, I wrote by candlelight at my little table. It was a fertile time, of thinking, making decisions for how my life would be, what I would become, what I had learned. I was becoming a man. My chin sprouted the beginnings of a beard and my voice, once a high soprano when I sang at school, was now deep.

By autumn, I had finished with my summer work at the farm, and started back at the library. It was an important year, my last year of schooling. The librarian brought me brochures for several universities offering architecture; all of course requiring me to leave the community and travel a great distance. We pored over the brochures together, finally choosing Cornell as the university I would apply to for a scholarship – that is, if my grades were good enough. New York seemed a long way to go, but I reasoned, it could be no more difficult than the three years I had spent at my tree house. I marvelled at how quickly the time had passed and all that I had learned and achieved.

Late one day I was walking home, enjoying the colours of the season. The leaves had turned and begun to drop. Red, gold, green, yellow splashes of colour filled my senses as the leaves swirled around in the breeze. The afternoon had closed in and it was almost dusk by the time I neared the crossroad. Ahead of me was a fully laden cart, pulled by two straining horses. As the driver reached the intersection and began to veer left, the horses reared; the cart tipped, trembled, overturned. I saw the driver thrown out, but he seemed unhurt when he landed against the bank. The horse on the left harness began to bolt, dragging the cart and the second horse along with him. The horses didn't go far, the weight of the cart impeding their progress.

I ran forward to help the driver and we both hurried to calm the animals. The driver unhitched the two geldings and turned them out on the side of the road. Then together we set about righting the cart and retrieving the fallen cargo, now spread across the ground.

It took some time for us to get his goods reloaded and tied down securely. Before putting the horses back into their harness, we walked back to the crossroads to investigate the cause of the problem, and found a rock on the side of the road. We surmised that the wheel of the cart must have caught against the rock as the driver turned. The driver was puzzled. Normally, he said, a rock wouldn't set the horses off. Perhaps an animal or something else had spooked the horse making it rear up and bolt. We searched around, although it was getting quite dark and the driver was anxious to be getting on his way again. As he was about to climb up onto the cart, he spied something in the ditch. At first glance, it looked like a pile of old clothing, but when the driver pulled at it, we found the pile to be a body.

It took some time for us to drag the body out. To my horror, when we turned the body over, I discovered it was my father. I stood in shock, staring down at him. All I could think about was the last time we had spoken, just a couple of months earlier. Suddenly I recalled the dream with my mother measuring something and this time I realised what she was trying to show me – time. It was time that she was indicating when she kept marking the tape near the end. She was telling me father was getting ready to leave, that it was his time.

The driver was very upset, that perhaps the wheel of the cart had hit the man and knocked him into the ditch. But the body was quite cold and stiff, and it seemed as though my father had been there for some time. I consoled him, saying that it was not his fault, before I ran to my old next-door neighbour. I banged on the door, taking him from his dinner, asking for his assistance, telling him what I had found. He came back with me straight away, pulling his small handcart. I carefully lifted my father from the ground. He weighed little in my arms, and I remembered the way he had carried my mother when he brought her to her chair on the porch. It was just the same. We laid my father's body on the cart and after some discussion, decided to take him back to his farmhouse, my old home. I offered the driver a bed for the night, as it was by now far too late for him to keep travelling, and the inn where he had intended to stop was still some distance.

I struggled to open the kitchen door and enter the house. The house was filthy, the kitchen filled with dirty dishes. The floor clearly hadn't been washed in I don't know how long, there was mould on the counter, and the range obviously hadn't been used recently.

My mother's beautiful raspberry velvet sofa in the space past the kitchen, the space she called her sitting room, was now dirty, damaged. It appeared to have become father's permanent bed.

So I laid him on it; a little man, shrunken in death. The neighbour invited the driver and me to his farmhouse to have a meal and a drink. After feeding the horses and putting them in the barn, we went next door.

While we ate, his wife went across to our farm to attend to laying out my father properly. I was grateful for her kindness; I would not have been able to do that. By the time we returned from our meal, father was clean, his hair and beard washed and trimmed. The farmer's wife had found father's best suit and dressed him in it, although now it was far too big for him. He looked much better than when I had carried him in, and at peace, somehow. She had attempted to clean the sofa, but given up, and asked me if I thought it would be better to lay him on the bed he and mother had shared, instead. I shook my head, and we left him there.

The driver took to the bed in the spare room, the one with the camphor box, and fell asleep almost instantly, his snores rattling the walls of the house.

I entered my old room for the first time in over three years. Nothing had changed, nothing had been moved. I think my father must have shut the door to my room and never gone in again. Dust lay heavy over everything, and I had to open the window and shake out the bedding before I could go to bed. I used the kitchen broom to take the worst of the dust off the desk and the chest of drawers after I swept the floor.

In the morning, the driver apologised again for the incident, thanked me for the bed, paid his respects to my father on the sofa, and went on his way. I walked to the doctor, to let him know that father had died, and to get the death certificate. Fortunately, he was at home when I reached his house. He greeted me kindly, and once I had explained the situation, gave me a ride back to the farm with him on his horse. After examining father carefully, he concluded that father must have fallen down drunk, passed out and died in the cold night air the previous night. He believed the horse might have kicked him further into the ditch when it shied, but he was definitely dead at the time that occurred. There was no reason to suspect any foul play. Really, he said, your father died of a broken heart. And he wrote *heart cessation* as the cause on the death certificate.

That day, several people came out to the farm bringing food and their condolences. The publican came, with whisky, and a barrel of ale on his wagon to have after the burial. He said he would close the bar, as everyone would most likely be coming here anyway. He told me that father hadn't been in to the saloon the day before, and he wondered what might have happened. Father had become his most regular guest. He said he had seen father off as usual at closing time, two nights ago and had commented that the moon was so full and bright father would have been able to see his way home easily. Although, he said, father had travelled that road so many times since mother died, he didn't need anything to light his way. His feet knew the route well. A fair number of travellers must have passed by the crossroads during the day, but not one had noticed him, sprawled across the edge of the road, half in the ditch. The pastor came to the house later in the morning to arrange for the burial, and later in the day the lawyer from the neighbouring township arrived in his carriage, bringing papers with him for me to sign, the deeds to the farm, and information about my parent's estates. When I asked him how he knew about father, he explained that the doctor had been in the town and they had met up unexpectedly. There was money from my mother, which father had never mentioned to me. I expect because I was just a boy, or maybe he had forgotten entirely about it. I think that perhaps both reasons were valid.

The near derelict farm was now mine, along with some money from my maternal grandparents, which the lawyer had held in trust for me, and the money father had left. Added to the sum from my mother, in all it was a tidy legacy, and I was surprised and pleased, as altogether the money provided more than enough to repair the farmhouse, plus a good contribution towards my university studies. Assuming that is, I was accepted somewhere.

It was time for me to make a decision. Should I return to the tree house in the forest that had become my home, or was it time for me to take my place back in the community and become more visible in the village. I mulled it over all that night, as I lay awake, thinking it all through, choosing one plan, then another, and in the morning had still not made up my mind.

The midday service for my father was well attended and the pastor took his time, no doubt pleased to have such a good turnout for his preaching. The gaping hole beside my mother received father's body and the men all took their turn to shovel the earth and cover the plain wooden box. I was first with the shovel. I heard the earth fall on the wood, such a final, mournful sound and my tears fell with it. I really was alone now.

I walked back to the farmhouse with my neighbours – the kindly farmer and his wife from across the road, and the two families who had lived each side of my family for so many years. The men had been at school with my father, and had such a lot of anecdotes about the things he got up to when young. The women in the community had cleaned the house from top to bottom, and set out good plain fare on the kitchen table. Even mother's raspberry sofa now looked almost good as new and with tears in my eyes I thanked the farmer's wife who had cleaned it so well. The sofa was much a strong memory of my mother, and so special; I knew that wherever I went in my adult life it would accompany me – even if only in my thoughts.

The cask of ale brought by the publican was opened and we farewelled father the way the community had for generations.

The afternoon was a time for remembering both my mother and father, and the people who came had many stories they recalled of happier times. I heard stories of my father's youth, of the time when he courted my mother, their marriage and their happiness together. It wasn't long before I learned that many of the neighbours knew where I was all along. Most of the men had been out in the forest from time to time over the last year or two and had seen my tree house. They were all astonished at what a young lad had created. They asked me how I had lived there, how I had built the house so high up in the first place. They laughed when I told them how I acquired the materials, especially the hen house door hinges and how I had convinced the men working at the sawmill to part with stuff. My stories about pulling up the windows, fixing the roof, hiding from the bear, must have sounded to the community like an imaginary tale, except they knew it was all true.

No one asked, or mentioned that they knew why I had left. I guess it must have been obvious, with my bruises and cuts. I talked at length about my lofty home high in the tree, and what I done, and my plans for the future. I told them how my Indian friend had saved my life and what he had taught me. And I praised the farmers and their wives, who gave me work, clothes and food.

The librarian came over. We are all so proud of you, she said. I looked at her in surprise. Whom did she mean by all? The community, she replied. We all worked together to get you through. I was astonished.

Over the next few hours, I learned that many families had helped to provide my food baskets during the three winters I was in the forest. I hadn't even noticed that some days the baskets would be different. The librarian said that the doctor and the publican had quietly given her funds to help ensure I could complete my schooling. I asked why she hadn't told me, and she said they had asked her not to, to let me find my own way.

She also said that she had written from time to time to my Aunt Sally to tell her how I was doing. Aunt was under the impression that neighbours were looking after me, and no one wanted to dissuade her. My aunt had sent money each year to help with my examination fees, and to provide my clothing. The librarian had passed the money to the neighbour for the clothes she presented to me each summer.

I wondered why I had never noticed men in the forest, keeping the area near my tree house monitored to help keep me safe. They told they had tended to wait until I had left the forest on the days I went into the village. Apparently, the bear incident the year before last had been quite unexpected; the blizzard had made it impossible for anyone to check out the area for a few weeks. When the men returned to the forest and saw the marks on the tree, they had feared for the worst and were most relieved when they saw me once again heading into the library. I learned that several of the men had also gone to talk with the local Indians, and my friend had told them that I was safe.

I thought I had managed my living arrangements so well all by myself, and now I was learning that I hadn't. The librarian hastened to reassure me. No, no one interfered, and people only offered what they wanted to. We were all so concerned for you, and are so impressed at the way you managed, flourished even. The way I had been cared for by so many people was a revelation to me. I may not have had my mother, but I had been mothered by several of the women. And, while I did have a father, he was not capable of looking out for me, and the neighbouring farmers had effectively been father figures for me. I stopped feeling that sense of loss and abandonment that had been part of my life for so long.

Someone brought their squeezebox and sang, and as people left that evening, shaking my hand, or in the case of the women, hugging me, I began to feel that I was home, that I was a part of the community again. I decided to stay.

Chapter Eight: Resurrection

Choosing to move back to the farm – leaving the tree house that had been my home for three years, and the place where I grew from a boy to a man – was bittersweet. While I knew it was the right decision, I had grown fond of my tiny home and become settled in my routines.

I went back to the tree several times over the next few weeks, each time returning with some of my belongings; my books, the preserves that I was so proud of and the few clothes I had. It was hard to let go, and I left everything I didn't need back in the tree house, thinking that come summer I'd go back for a while. But winter was drawing closer, and that year was the last chance I would have to achieve highly in my final studies. I considered returning to the schoolhouse for my lessons, but after discussing options with the librarian, chose to continue with my solitary study at the library. Living at the farmhouse meant a shorter distance to travel each day, and I extended my time at the library from four days each week to five. The curriculum this year was full and often I took advantage of the school bus in the morning, as it enabled me to spend more time at my studies.

As I had ceased trapping since I returned to the farming community, I needed food baskets even more that winter, and like magic they were always on the mailbox waiting for me. I was so grateful. The contents of my baskets became my main meal again as I managed my studies, and undertook the urgent repairs necessary on the farmhouse.

Father had let the house fall into disrepair and it needed a huge amount done, including roof repairs to stop the leaks dribbling rusty water from the guttering down inside the wall of my old bedroom, staining the wallpaper and puddling on the wooden floor. I decided to move my bed into the kitchen, and close off the rest of the house. It was easier to heat the smaller space and my bedroom was unusable, but mostly I think I chose to do that because I had got so used to my tiny home that the farmhouse seemed too big. I built a large bookcase with a cupboard beside it in the kitchen to house my books and my clothes, and lived there happily. The one thing I loved best about being back home was the inside bathroom and the big bath. I had sorely missed warm water to bathe in, and I was grateful that my former excursions up and down the rope ladder each day were now just a memory. I often heated up the water in the tank from the wood range and enjoyed a long soak, even though the whole of me couldn't quite fit in, and my feet stuck out the end of the tub.

I created a plan to repair the farmhouse, measuring and drawing up my design and purchasing materials with some of the money from my grandparents. The fences and the barn would have to wait till the summer, but over the winter, when I wasn't studying, I worked on the house, room by room and found such satisfaction. I knew my decision to study architecture was the right one for me.

I laughed at the state of the hen house, the source of much of my treehouse materials, and the one outside job I did undertake was to pull down the old ramshackle shed and build a new one. I thought to buy some chickens in the spring and wanted it to be ready if I did go ahead with my purchase.

In June, I sat my final exams. The wait again seemed endless, more than a month this time, and it was fortunate my summer work kept me so busy that I had little time to brood about whether or not my dedication to my studies would bring me the desired results. When I learned I had passed with distinction, I applied for a scholarship at Cornell to study architecture and with the help of the librarian, I completed my application, submitting with it the drawings of the tree house and my plans for the farmhouse. At the librarian's suggestion, I did not mention that I had lived in the tree house, nor that I had not actually been in a classroom environment for my last four year's study. Instead, I responded to the questions about living circumstances using the farmhouse. I did state my parents were both deceased, in the required essay outlining the reasons for wanting a scholarship, and I wrote about the alterations to the farmhouse that I actually had made over the winter months since I moved back into the community.

For the next four weeks, I focused on the external repairs to the farmhouse. I pulled off all the old siding, not only the boards that were rotten, and stuffed wool into the framing as insulation before nailing on the new wood. The neighbouring farmers came to look at what I was doing, asking questions about why I would waste wool and why didn't I just replace the rotten boards with new ones, rather than replacing everything. They ended up staying to help and to take on my ideas. We would have lively discussions over a beer after we finished the work for the day, and I'd draw out my ideas on paper for them to take away. With the neighbours' help, I transformed most of the farmhouse that summer.

In July, I received a letter from Cornell, inviting me for an interview. I was thrilled to have earned this first level of selection, but was also somewhat nervous. New York seemed a very long way away and it was impossible for me to comprehend what it would be like to live and study there.

The librarian kindly offered to travel with me and I accepted with alacrity. We wrote for a copy of the Cornell Daily Sun, a newspaper that we thought would surely provide advertisements for suitable accommodation and places to eat.

We obtained seats on a train to Fort Kent. My first experience on a train, it was slow and basic, but the views of the river and the countryside from the train were wonderful. We overnighted at a small hotel near the railway station before boarding a train the following day on the new railway line to Bangor, where we changed to yet another train to take us to the port on the river. Once we finally boarded the boat in Searsport for our journey all the way to New York City I was greatly relieved; fortunately the sailing was smooth, the water calm and the weather clear. I wrote in my journal constantly, carefully describing the sights that were all so new to me – the bustling crowds, shops, noise, sights and smells of the towns we passed through. It was a busy coastal route and I spent the time when I put away my pen and notebook out on the deck looking around at the many boats travelling up and down the river and plying the coast. When our vessel finally moored in New York, we had taken more than a week to complete the journey from the farm. The difference in the environment was startling to me, that first time. I almost felt like we had arrived on another planet. The librarian laughed when I mentioned that to her.

By the time we reached the accommodation we had booked, it was late in the day and after a brief meal, I excused myself to return to my room to sleep. The accommodation at the hotel was satisfactory. In addition, it appeared to be a favourite place for students to eat and in the evening the dining room was full. The noise of all the conversations at the same time, of young men earnestly debating and their easy cheerful banter intoxicated me and I so wanted to become a part of it.

I took a walk around the town following day. It was very hot, and the noise, the hustle, the sheer number of people overwhelmed me. The librarian was far more familiar with the sights and sounds of a city. She was even comfortable walking around without an escort, she said, but I didn't allow that and made sure to walk with her.

I noted with dismay that the clothing worn by males in the city appeared quite different to my garb and I was worried that I would look out of place at my scholarship interview, scheduled for the afternoon of the next day. However, I was obliged to wear what I had brought with me.

I was up early the following morning, to prepare myself for the trial I felt sure was ahead. I arrived at the designated place with plenty of time to spare, and found myself a seat among the other potential candidates awaiting their interviews. As I looked around my heart sank. I was correct. I stuck out like a sore toe. My clothes were so out of place I almost got up and left. But I heard my mother whisper don't give up now, not after you have come all this way, and I resettled myself, resigned to whatever outcome occurred.

Across from my seat was a young woman with a very large hat. What little of her hair I could see appeared be dark brown. She looked at me shyly with soft brown eyes, and smiled, mouthing good luck when I stood after they called out my name. I smiled back hesitantly, wondering who she was, and turned to follow the man who had appeared beside me.

The interview panel comprised four men. They looked stern, forbidding, and my heart sank further. However, the youngest man, perhaps ten years my senior, smiled as he asked me to sit, and introduced himself, along with the rest of the panel. For more than thirty minutes, the panel members asked me a series of wide-ranging questions, covering my general education, my family, where I was from, my aspirations. A copy of my examination results sat on the table in front of the senior professor and he looked it over carefully while the others questioned me. At one stage he interjected, interrupting another of the professors, asking me to discuss my tree house, and if I thought it was feasible that a person might truly be able to live in such a dwelling, or if it was fantasy. My response to his question regarding the ability to live in a tree house was limited to my view that I was sure it was quite possible. He further asked if I believed that stuffing wool into the framing of a house would actually keep it warmer in winter and cooler in summer. I hastened to explain that I actually had done that with the farmhouse earlier in the year, and not only was I convinced it worked effectively; I had managed to persuade several of my neighbours to consider undertaking a similar course of action. No doubt egged on by their wives, who would appreciate more warmth, I suggested. There was no responding smile to my attempt at humour. I wondered if that would be a mark against me.

I left the room, when the committee dismissed me, feeling most discouraged. The young woman who had smiled at me was no longer in her seat, and quite unreasonably I felt disappointed. When I emerged into the bright sunlight, the librarian was waiting for me. Come along, she said, we'll have lunch and then go sightseeing. That cheered me up somewhat, and off we went.

The invitation to the interview stipulated that applicants must make themselves available for three days following the initial interview, in case the committee wished to recall a candidate for further questioning. During that time, I located a tailor not far from the hotel, on East State Street, and went in to order a new suit of clothes. Even if I was unsuccessful in obtaining a scholarship, I had made up my mind that I would work and save until I had sufficient to pay for my own schooling and could apply again for admission as a regular student. I was pleasantly surprised that the tailor was not at all perturbed by the outdated style and less than perfect condition of my clothing, and after asking my requirements, set about measuring me for a four-button city suit in the style adopted by many of the students.

As the tailor circled me with his tape measure, he gave me good advice on a suitable student wardrobe. I was most grateful for his concern. He suggested that I purchase a black silk string tie for dress occasions, and a couple of handsome broad ties, made of silk also, for classes. I picked one coloured scarlet and plum and a second with a small amount of purple on a darker background. In addition to the suit, I bought four shirts together with the proper collars, and he recommended that I shop further along East State Street for suitable shoes. I looked down at my feet in my country boots and agreed that would be my next stop. On the way there, I passed an ice cream parlour advertising a sundae and went in to partake of one, my very first. The coolness on my tongue and the sweet flavours made the sundae an instant hit. After lingering in the cool air of the ice cream parlour for some time, I finally took myself further along the wide street to a department store where I purchased a pair of city shoes. I hoped that if Cornell recalled me for a second interview, my new suit might be ready, but if not, at least I had a better shirt and collar, and shoes that were more suitable. I worried that I had spent a fair bit of the money I had brought with me improving my appearance, but was confident I had used my cash wisely and that none of my purchases would go unused.

Alas, I did not receive a recall letter, and when I went back to read the lists of admissions my name was not there. However, to my great pleasure, the young woman in the big hat was standing near the entrance of the admissions hall, wearing yet another huge device on her head. I smile tentatively and she beamed. Were you accepted, she asked? I shook my head. Me neither. The admission requirements for women are so difficult, but I'm definitely going to try again next year. What about you? I said I thought I might, but that I lived a long way away. She seemed interested enough in where I lived and we talked for some time, finally exchanging names. She mentioned where she lived in the city, not far from the college of architecture. In fact, almost close enough to walk each day, that was, once she was accepted, she laughed. Except females must board in the college dorms, she said so she would have even less distance to get to class.

With reluctance, I eventually bid her farewell and left, feeling a sense of exhilaration. Her warm brown eyes enchanted me. She seemed such a lovely young woman and I hoped we might keep in touch somehow. At least, I now knew her name and where she lived. I thought that perhaps I might write to her, if her parents approved.

I walked about the town the next two days, waiting for the tailor to complete my suit, and hoping that I might again come across "my" young woman in the hat, as I had taken to referring to her in my mind. Unfortunately, I did not see her, and soon it was time to embark on the long trip back home.

By the time the librarian and I were finally back in our community there was a formal letter waiting for me from the university to say the committee had declined my application. It was not a complete rejection though, as the dean recommended I reapply for a scholarship the following year. I intended to do just that and thought, next time, if I obtained an interview, at least I had the right clothes to wear. And perhaps I might even get an opportunity to develop a friendship with the young woman with the big hats and the beautiful brown eyes. Annie. Her name was Annie.

I decided to ask if there might be a vacancy at my old school for a teacher. That would provide me with a regular income and some teaching experience, which I could include on my next application. The head teacher accepted my offer with great eagerness, and I commenced teaching in the fall.

I wrote an initial letter to Annie, with a cover letter to her parents, explaining who I was, and asking for permission to correspond. I got that idea from the librarian, when I mentioned I had met someone. It was obviously the right approach, as three weeks later I received my first missive from her. Our correspondence flourished over the winter, keeping the mailman busy delivering letters to the farmhouse, and picking up my replies. On days I expected a letter I would rush to get home as quickly as possible after school finished, so I could check the mailbox.

The head teacher had assigned me woodwork, science and English classes and I found I enjoyed teaching all three subjects very much. I found that in teaching, I continued learning, not only to answer the questions the students posed, but also to further develop and deepen my own knowledge. The winter term passed quickly, and once spring was in the air I decided to take my older students out to the tree house, to show them where and how I had lived for three years.

We set out one sunny day. I was used to the walk and didn't think about the distance at all, but a few of the students who lived close to the village found it somewhat tiring. By the time we got to the end of the road, three of the five were slowing down. Not much further to go I reassured them, and it's cool in the trees. We reached my tree and I pulled out the rope ladder from where I had hidden it: in a deep fissure in the bark. I could see concerned looks among the students – are we really going to climb right up there? Just on that rope ladder? One asked. Yes, I replied, get a move on. But what if it breaks? It won't I said confidently. I've been up and down it so many times and never had a problem. With doubtful looks on their faces the students climbed up one by one.

Once they had mastered the rope ladder and stepped off onto the deck of my old home the students were, without exception, excited and amazed. The tree house looked somewhat forlorn after having been unoccupied over the winter, and I hoped that no predators had gained entrance whilst I was absent. I unlocked the padlock I had used to secure the door – and ushered my guests into my tiny home. Everything was just as I had left it, and five students stared around, mesmerised. Did you really truly live here? All alone? In the dark? With wild animals? The questions came thick and fast. I paused, listened, and marvelled myself. How had I managed this, a child of twelve? Now it seemed fantastic, but at the time I had first moved in the drive to leave home had over-ridden any other consideration.

I showed them what I had built, how I had made the extensions, my shelves, my bed – of which I was so proud – the fireplace and cooking rack, and the safe outside. I talked to them about the bear and showed his claw marks, still clearly visible in the bark. They stood and looked at everything with awe.

Eventually, it was time to lock up the tree house and return to school. I made the students promise not to go out to the tree house on their own, or take others out there. For safety, this time I detached the ladder from the tethering rope and took it with me. It was an easy job to reconnect it to the rope, but I was sure the absence of any way to get up to the tree house would ensure it remained mine, and out of reach to anyone else. I did not want to be responsible for harm befalling any other person, nor was I keen to have anyone touching my precious things.

Over the year, I continued to work on repairing and modernising the farmhouse, and documenting my progress. I was pleased to have had the opportunity to go through a winter in my insulated house to prove conclusively that the wool stuffing was indeed effective and I hoped the further work I had undertaken on the building would be a mark in my favor should I be offered an interview at Cornell again in the summer. I created a chart to record the inside and outside temperatures each day, as a way to prove to myself that the wool did indeed provide a measure of insulation. I also I asked the farmer next door to record the interior and exterior temperature at his farmhouse, and as we compared notes each day, the variations became quite clear. I had an instant convert.

Several of the neighbouring farmers had decided to use some of their wool in the same manner, and I was more than happy to repay the help they had given me by taking them through the process. The farmers' wives remarked on how cool the house stayed in the summer, and they certainly noticed the increased warmth in the winter.

I resubmitted my application for a scholarship to Cornell in May of the next year and again included with my application the sketches of the tree house and scale drawings of the farmhouse changes. This time I was able to add information about the success of the wool as insulation, as well as a testimonial from the head teacher covering my year of teaching. And, in further support of my application, I enclosed letters of recommendation from several farmers, all mentioning my innovations and the ideas and support I had offered or provided. I hoped the testimony from the farmer who worked on the temperature chart with me would prove a compelling argument in my favour. I was determined to make the best possible impression this time.

Finally, I sent a second application as an unsupported scholar, in the hope that one way or the other I would have a place in the school of architecture come September.

It was a much more difficult wait this time. Although my days were taken up with teaching, and my evenings and days off with work on the farmhouse as well as out in the fields, I worried that neither application would be successful and I that would have to think of a new way to realise my dream. I kept writing to Annie, and I knew she was just as concerned that I would not be accepted – or that she would not.

In June, I was thankfully, once again offered an interview. I prepared for the trip carefully, packing my new and as-yet unworn clothes – after trying everything on to ensure they still fitted.

I repeated the journey into New York City, travelling alone this time, with the confidence of having taken the trip before, and feeling sure that I could find my way around. Getting there seemed so much easier and I arrived ready and excited. Annie and her parents were waiting for me at the dock when the boat tied up and I was so glad to see her, and meet her family. Pleased also, that I had changed out of my country clothes into my new city attire before the boat had reached the landing, just in case Annie was there. I doubted her parents would have looked upon me so favourably if I was still wearing my old clothes.

Fortunately, this year I was one of the first applicants called for an interview, and I felt for all the others sitting in that cavernous room. I wondered how many were waiting for an interview for the second time, like me, but to my unschooled eye it seemed as if they were all younger than I was and fresh from school. Annie's interview was scheduled for later in the day, but she came in the morning to wish me luck, and sat with me in the big hall as I waited. I felt very proud and comfortable sitting with her and pleased that I wasn't on my own. Her hat this time was somewhat smaller although just as elegant and certainly framed her face quite beautifully. When I mentioned the fact, she blushed and laughed and said fashions changed every year.

The interview process was far less daunting, and I felt more confident that this time I might be successful. The interview panel was the same as before, and surprisingly, all four greeted me kindly.

The senior professor declared that since they had already learned of my background and career plans, they wished to focus on my architectural and building work over the last year. On two occasions they referred to testimonials from one neighbour or another, and appeared impressed with the report from the headmaster, especially concerning the woodwork programme I had put in place for my students. My detailed study and charts on temperature variations also merited quite some discussion. The interview lasted almost an hour this time, and as I left the room, the youngest member of the panel walked out with me and shook my hand. The world needs innovation like yours, he said, and asked if he might know where I was accommodated. When I replied I was lodging at the Ithaca Hotel, he nodded. I relayed the conversation to

Annie, still sitting cheerfully after that long wait, and she felt convinced this was surely an indication that my application would be successful.

I in turn waited with her in the afternoon and while her interview took place, and then walked with her back to her home, a large gracious building surrounded by tall trees, lush grass and well-tended flowerbeds. It made my farmhouse look shabby and unkempt, despite all the new work that I had done. Her parents had invited me for dinner, a formal affair and I felt somewhat out of place. However, they treated me kindly, and as if I was an honoured guest, and I finally found myself enjoying the food, the company and the conversation. Her three brothers, all older than her, were great fun and kept the conversation lively.

After breakfast in the hotel dining room next day, I decided to take in some of the sights I had missed the previous year. As I was about to leave the building, the concierge called out that he had a special delivery for me. The thick cream envelope was familiar, and I closed my eyes for a moment, with a fast beating heart, praying that the letter would say I had been selected for a recall, before lifting the flap and withdrawing the contents. It took me a moment to read the correspondence, and then I had to read it again. No, not a recall – I had been accepted on a full scholarship for my entire four year course of study.

I was speechless. Instead of going outside, I ran back to my room and wrote out a telegram to the librarian informing her of my great good fortune. I then rushed to Annie's home to tell her, unheeding of propriety. It was fortunate for me that Annie's parents, with their three sons, had become used to extravagant gestures from young men and were delighted with my news. The following day, Annie received her acceptance as well. She had not applied for a scholarship, as her family were well able to fund her studies. Celebrations were in order, and that night I again spent a very pleasant evening with Annie and her family. I had been somewhat surprised, but very impressed the previous year, that Annie's parents were so encouraging about her tertiary studies. Now that I understood their strong views about the importance of education for women, a position I concurred with, I happily engaged in a number of serious discussions covering all manner of topics. It was late when I finally bid Annie goodnight.

This time, the three days that had passed so slowly the previous year flew by and too soon I was boarding a steamer back to Bangor, waving Annie goodbye. We had permission from her parents to spend quite a lot of time together, which we took advantage of, as Annie showed me the city. We attended the opera, and a summer gala. I did not venture much of my personal desires for the future to Annie, considering it somewhat premature, but I felt that she knew and reciprocated my affection for her. I spent the return journey making plans. Plans about the farmhouse, knowing I had to get as much completed as possible before university started. Plans on what I would do afterwards. Would I return to the community as I had previously thought I would, and continue my work there? Would it provide me with enough work to support a family, should I be lucky enough to have one? Where I might go to practice my profession if I did move to another location?

Plans that I hoped would all include a life with Annie.

Over that last summer in the community, I completed the external work on the farmhouse. The long dry sunny days gave me plenty of time to finish all the work and the house once again stood proud with white painted trim against a soft blue, my mother's favourite colour, and a shiny new roof. Summer roses of blush pink once again clambered up the side of the verandah and peeped in the upstairs windows; cornflowers, daisies and red poppies grew everywhere in the yard. I had been lavish with my seeds, wanting an ocean of colour, and nature had rewarded me abundantly. From a catalogue, I purchased new wicker rocking chairs for the porch, and placed on them the brightly covered pillows and scarlet throw brought to me as a gift by the farmer's wife across the way. She said she thought my mother would have loved what I had done. I felt sure mother was there and saw it all. I imagined her in the rocking chair, listening to the birds, the summer scents all around her. It felt good.

I finally gathered enough courage to enter my parent's room one evening. The door had stayed shut since I moved back in, and I suspected, ever since my father had chosen mother's sofa as his place of refuge each night. While I had considered what changes I might make to the room, I had never gone in. Even the necessary repairs to the window I accomplished from the outside, up a long ladder wired to the roof for safety.

When I opened the door I could smell my mother's perfume, and suddenly it was if I were a small boy again. Mother was sitting at her dressing table holding the cut glass bottle that still sat there, spraying a tiny drop in the base of her throat. I was sitting on the floor, looking up at her. Mother looked down at me, her face alight and full of love and I heard her whisper my strong, brave, wonderful boy. Your father and I are so proud of you. I sat on the chair in the window, just remembering, feeling her arms around me, her voice whispering in my ear and I was truly happy and at peace.

It was quite some time before I eventually rose and began the task of clearing and cleaning the room. In the back of the wardrobe I came across a box containing a package of letters tied with a ribbon, letters my father had written to my mother before they were married. I stopped to read them. It was evident how much he had loved her even then. In the same box were other letters, that father had written to mother when she became ill. He thanked her for the joy she had brought to his life, for the gift of a son, and so much more. He wrote down everything in their marriage that had made his life so happy and contented. Mother must have loved to read those letters I thought. Perhaps he read them to her in bed at night, in the cosy room with the candle glow. Their love was an inspiration to me. I hoped that someday I would be so lucky in love.

I spent a long time reading all the letters. I knew mother wouldn't mind. Maybe they had been left for me. Maybe father had forgotten them. I chose to believe that he had left them for me, deliberately. Now, as an adult, I began to understand better the depth of father's grief and how it took over his life. I was so devastated when mother died. I wondered why I had not realised, not considered, how distraught father must have been. He was left behind to raise a boy on his own, a boy who would remind him of his lost love every day. A boy who looked so like his beloved wife that he was too sad to face me. I knew I looked like her – I saw her, every time I peered in a mirror. Her eyes, her nose, the way my hair fell over my forehead in the same way hers did, imprinted on my young man's face. After reading the letters, when my mother made it so clear when she whispered to me that they were together again, and happy, I knew I could forgive father for his lack of care for me, and for his violence and anger towards me.

I cleaned and scrubbed the room until it shone. I repainted the walls the same pale pink mother had loved – the colour that echoed the roses peering in the window; and the ceiling a sharp white, after removing years of cobwebs. I washed the bedding and hung out the mattress and the feather comforter on the resurrected clothesline; the new forked pole I had cut pushing everything high into the air to capture the breeze. I polished the windows and the mirror and buffed the bedhead and the dressing table until the cherry wood gleamed the way mother had always kept it.

I cleared out all of mother's clothes, and those of father's, too. Nothing of father's fitted me; I was now a good seven or eight inches taller than he had been. There were others in the community who were grateful to have them. I put the package of letters, with the broad pink ribbon rewrapped around them, back in the box just as mother – or maybe even father – had left it, and returned it to the bottom of the wardrobe.

Soon, it was time to leave the farmhouse and embark on the next part of my life.

Before I left the community I took another trip into the forest. I had not seen my Indian friend for some time, and I missed him. I walked far into the trees, towards the north east, towards his settlement. He had taken me there, but I hadn't found my own way before. I had my compass, and set a steady course, eventually finding my way to the small valley that was their summer home. He was pleased to see me, and I explained as best I could that I was travelling away to study, but that I would return each summer. He journeyed all the way back with me to the road, past my tree house, and he promised to keep a watch over it for me. I gave him the key to the padlock, in case he wanted to spend time there. On the softy bed he grinned, and I laughed. I thanked him for his care of me, and for all he had taught me.

He took my hand as I said goodbye, and wished me luck, before silently disappearing into the trees.

I rose early the morning of my departure, the air still and the leaves just starting their autumnal descent. My trunk was packed, and my satchel with everything I would need to start my new studies waited beside it at the kitchen door.

I walked along the road to the cemetery, to where mother and father were buried beside each other. I brought posies of red poppies and blue cornflowers and laid one beside each headstone. It was time for me to say goodbye, and to say all the other words I had held back for so many years.

I knelt down beside my parents under the tree on the small knoll and poured out my heart. I told father how very much I loved him, and how grateful I was for his tender care before mother died. I said I understood his pain. And I asked for his forgiveness, for my leaving him alone and lonely. He had lost his treasured son, the night I walked away into the forest, not just his beloved wife. No wonder he took refuge in a bottle and died of a broken heart.

The boy that I once was had gone, and in his place stood a man. A man with a lot of knowledge, about life, about living, but with plenty more to learn. A quiet, thinking, kind person to whom people were drawn, with an inner strength that it seemed others recognised. A man about to set out on his next stage in life.

When I reached the railway station I was astonished. It appeared that everyone had come to see me off on my journey. I was overwhelmed at the kindness and generosity of everyone. People brought me food for the journey and cards wishing me well for the future and success in my studies, and from my students at the school, small notes of thanks. The publican brought me three bottles of beer, to quench my thirst on the journey. The doctor came, with advice on keeping healthy in the dirty city air and not succumbing to the ways of some of the less driven students. I laughed and assured him I was at university to work, not play. The farmers all came to shake my hand, thanking me for helping them, and saying they expected to see me back with stories to tell and new learning to impart to them, at the summer recess each year. Those men – and their wives – were the ones who needed thanking for all the help they had given me over the years. They had truly kept me alive. My neighbours from across the road promised to keep an eye on the farmhouse, in exchange for the extra grazing on my fields, and I knew that the farm was in good hands. The last person to greet me before I boarded the train was the librarian. She hugged me fiercely, and told me she expected regular progress letters and no less than merit each year of my studies. I knew she would always be a treasured, special person in my life, however long or short it was.

I made myself a promise as the train pulled away from the station and left behind the life and people that I knew and cared for.

I would return. Each summer during the four years of my studies, of course, but afterwards, too. I would do everything I could to help and support others in the community the way I had been cared for. I would bring Annie, if she'd have me, and we would make a life together, here.

www.ingramcontent.com/pod-product-compliance
Lightning Source LLC
Chambersburg PA
CBHW071325130626
46556CB00004B/1751

* 9 7 8 0 9 9 4 1 1 6 1 0 9 *